SEARCHING
FOR TERRY
PUNCHOUT

A NOVEL

"*Searching for Terry Punchout* does just what its title promises—packs a punch. Readers will be knocked out by Hellard's dry and bittersweet humour as protagonist Adam attempts to navigate a return to the 'charming' small-town and father he bid adios to years ago. Hilarious and heartbreaking—an excellent debut novel."

— THEANNA BISCHOFF, AUTHOR OF *CLEAVAGE*, *SWALLOW*, AND *LEFT*

"It doesn't take much to get me to read a novel featuring hockey and a guy named Terry, but Tyler Hellard's stellar debut hit me like an errant stick to the head. A big story set in a small town, by turns funny and sad, moving and melancholy, *Searching for Terry Punchout* stays with you long after the final buzzer. Masterful."

—TERRY FALLIS, TWO-TIME WINNER OF THE STEPHEN LEACOCK MEDAL FOR HUMOUR

"Funny, quirky, sad, and sweet. *Searching for Terry Punchout* is a story of friendship and family, of hockey heroes and small-town hangovers, of Zamboni lessons, and thrift store beauty queens. Highly recommended!"

— WILL FERGUSON, AUTHOR OF *THE SHOE ON THE ROOF*

"Tyler Hellard has created a thoughtful, warm-hearted, and deeply human sports tale, one that will resonate with any read`er who has wondered if you can ever really go home again. *Searching For Terry Punchout* is a vivid portrait of small town hockey life, of fathers and sons, of feeling left behind and leaving things behind, of clinging to glory and grasping for meaning. With this strong debut, Hellard makes sense of what home really means, and in doing so reveals how close we actually are to the people and places that can often feel so far away."

— STACEY MAY FOWLES, AUTHOR OF *BASEBALL LIFE ADVICE*

"Tyler Hellard's *Searching for Terry Punchout* is utterly complete and heartbreakingly authentic. If all the rinks in small-town Canada and the game of hockey itself were to suddenly disappear from the earth, they could be reconstructed from the blueprint that is this excellent novel. And if you know the game at all at its grassroots, you'll recognize characters from these pages and never look at them the same way again."

— GARE JOYCE, AUTHOR OF *THE CODE*, *THE BLACK ACE*, AND *EVERY SPRING A PARADE*

"*Searching for Terry Punchout* is a funny, profane, charming romp of a novel about hockey culture in small-town Canada, which would be enough to recommend it on its own. But it's also an engaging and insightful look at the way men try and mostly fail to be honest and emotional in their relationships with other men, and that makes it a must-read."

— CHRIS TURNER, AUTHOR OF *THE PATCH* AND *THE GEOGRAPHY OF HOPE*

SEARCHING FOR TERRY PUNCHOUT

A NOVEL

Tyler Hellard

Invisible Publishing
Halifax & Picton

Library and Archives Canada Cataloguing in Publication

Hellard, Tyler, 1978-, author
    Searching for Terry Punchout / Tyler Hellard.

Issued in print and electronic formats.
ISBN 978-1-988784-10-6 (softcover). – ISBN 978-1-988784-14-4 (EPUB)

    I. Title.

PS8615.E4365S43 2018   C813'.6   C2018-904414-4
                                                C2018-904415-2

Edited by Leigh Nash
Cover and interior design by Megan Fildes | Typeset in Laurentian
With thanks to type designer Rod McDonald

Printed and bound in Canada

Invisible Publishing | Halifax & Picton
www.invisiblepublishing.com

Published with the generous assistance of the Canada Council for the Arts and the Ontario Arts Council.

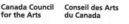

The male is not less the soul nor more, he too is in his place,
He too is all qualities, he is action and power,
The flush of the known universe is in him,
Scorn becomes him well, and appetite and
    defiance become him well,
The wildest largest passions, bliss that is utmost,
    sorrow that is utmost become him well, pride is for him,
The full-spread pride of man is calming and
    excellent to the soul,
Knowledge becomes him, he likes it always, he brings
    every thing to the test of himself,
Whatever the survey, whatever the sea and
    the sail he strikes soundings at last only here,
(Where else does he strike soundings except here?)

— WALT WHITMAN, "I SING THE BODY ELECTRIC"

It's always been a part of the game. The fans love fighting.
The players don't mind. The coaches like the fights.
What's the big deal?

— DON CHERRY

This bed is my reward after three long days of driving. My body is stiff and aches with exhaustion. When I collapsed here, I was sure the bed would swallow me and I'd sleep for days, but the groaning springs, the mattress that smells of stale rust, and my own creeping anxiety won't let me settle. If I'm being honest, it's probably just the anxiety.

The Goode Night Inn sits on the edge of Pennington in northeastern Nova Scotia. It's a motel for tourists: better people from better places who find musty mattresses quaint and charming. Every surface in the room is covered with lighthouses and mayflower patterns and decorative shells. There's a coffee table made from an old lobster trap. Being here makes my chest tight, East Coast kitsch fuelling my panic.

I remember the people who own this place, or rather, I remember their son, Mark. Four years older than me, Mark Goode was leaving junior high as I arrived, and it was the same in high school. Talented, handsome, and popular, Mark never seemed like a real person. He was a Class President 1992 photo in our high school's front hall and a name filling trophies in the glass case at the rink. Mark was captain of the Pennington Royals back when I believed playing for the Royals was all anyone could hope to achieve in life. Where had Mark Goode ended up? Wherever he is, I'm sure he has success and money and a pretty wife with whom he's made a dozen pretty babies. How could someone like him not?

The motel ceiling is dirty, but even the dirt feels quaint. I can't say for sure how long I've been staring at it. This is not where I belong. In fact, cutting out war zones and leper colonies and the really cold parts of Manitoba, this is the last place in the world I want to be. Pennington is a rot. It's a stink that sticks to you like smoke from a campfire. It's a glue trap; to escape means chewing off your own limbs.

I might be exaggerating, but only a little. I'm in the throes of an existential crisis, which can bring on certain failures of perspective.

"How long will you be staying with us?" Mrs. Goode asked me from behind the counter in the motel office when I checked in.

"I don't know. A week?" Would I really be here for a week? Maybe more. Probably more. Indefinitely? Fuck.

Mrs. Goode raised her eyebrows when she read the name on my credit card, then furrowed them as she tried to solve the puzzle of my family tree. Lineage matters around here. She knew my stock was Macallister, though not which sort of Macallister.

"You're Vivian's boy."

Rats. Besides my father's name, I also have my mother's eyes.

"Yes."

"Your mother and I used to run around together," Mrs. Goode said, holding her hands over her heart. "She was a lovely woman."

I pulled my lips back in a way that wasn't wholly a smile, head down, eyes up, like a four-year-old who's shit his pants and isn't sure if he's in trouble or not. Mrs. Goode, showing incredible kindness, let me off easy by handing over my room key without more discussion.

Pennington is a small town the way all towns in Nova Scotia are small. In the summer, it smells like salt, and in the winter it snows that wet, heavy Maritime snow—heart-attack snow, they call it. Everybody knows of everybody else and their business. The same guy has been mayor for thirty years and will be until he doesn't want it or, more likely, he drops dead, at which time his son will probably take over. It's a town that thrives on routine and expectation and neighbourly kindness. There are hundreds of towns just like this—Pennington, Pugwash, Tatamagouche, Antigonish, Pictou. The specifics don't matter.

I need a drink. Maybe two. The Goode Night Inn doesn't keep a stocked mini-bar. It feels late—in a Nova Scotia November, the sun sets shortly after lunch and doesn't come up again until May—but my watch says it's not quite nine o'clock. Actually, it says it's not quite six o'clock because I haven't spun it forward from Calgary time yet. I definitely need a drink. Probably two. It's the only thing that will keep me from getting back into my truck and driving three more days to, well, anywhere else. I have nowhere to be, but I also can't sit here anymore marinating in my own overwrought tension.

I dial the number to Sunshine Cabs from memory, surprising myself after all these years. Sunshine is two cars driven in shifts by a handful of guys, one of whom arrives in front of the motel in an old Monte Carlo about five minutes after I call. The cab's interior reeks, a combination of the cigarette the driver is smoking now and the two hundred thousand that came before it. There's no meter, Sunshine Cabs use a flat fee: five dollars inside town limits, seven to the rural roads.

"Where to?" the driver asks.

"A bar," I say. "Pat's Pub, I guess."

He looks at me through the rear-view mirror. "Pub closes at nine on Wednesdays."

Shit. "Are there any bars open?"

He considers my question for a second. "I s'pose J.J.'s will do ya."

I've never heard of it, so it must have opened in the last ten years. "Sure, take me there."

He pulls out of the lot of the Goode Night Inn and, four and a half minutes later, into the lot of the Pennington Recreation Centre. The rec centre, as its name hints, isn't a bar. I spent a lot of time here as a kid and, from the outside, the building doesn't seem to have changed at all. I make no effort to either pay or get out of the cab, and the driver eventually turns in his seat to look at me. Time and experience and smoke have weathered his face. I can tell this is a man who knows things—life lessons learned first-hand through circumstance and questionable decisions. I am in need of sage words of comfort and direction. He takes a long pull on his cigarette, the cherry glowing in dark silence.

"Bar's upstairs. Five bucks."

As sage words go, they're a bit lacking in comfort, but at least the direction is clear.

·

Built in the mid-1980s, the Pennington Rec Centre houses the local hockey rink, a small canteen, and eight lanes of five-pin bowling. The rink, Macallister Stadium, seats about four thousand, a little less than half the population of the entire town, and used to be filled for each of the twenty-eight home games the Pennington Royals play each season. The bowling alley, on the other hand, was used almost exclusively by Rotary Club members and kids' birthday parties, and, truth be told, not even very many of those.

Since I was last here, the guts of the building have been renovated: the floor in the lobby upgraded from brown tile to blue tile, the old trophy case replaced with a newer, bigger trophy case. The box office—a small booth in the middle of the room—is dark and empty. About ten feet behind it, the double doors that lead into the rink are closed, though I can hear the echo of pucks banging off boards from inside, likely from a practising team or beer-league game, at this time of night. The biggest wall in the lobby has an old mural of hockey players—kids and seniors, some wearing old brown gear, others with more modern stuff. I think it's supposed to represent hockey through the years or com- munity spirit or whatever, but the guy who painted it was bad at faces so all the adults look like sad tropical birds, the kids like deranged cherubs. The only goalie in the image, standing to the far side of the wall, has had half his body covered with a large vinyl sign. Blocky red letters spell out "J.J.'s Sports Bar" and "Five Dollar Jugs Before Every Home Game." There's an arrow pointing to a dark staircase tucked around the corner.

Up the stairs and through a door, I find the bar. The space used to be a Legion-sponsored room where veterans could smoke cigars and watch hockey through a bank of windows looking out onto the ice, above the scoreboard at the visitors' end. Add a bar, some tables and chairs, stick a pool table in the corner, and presto—a perfectly acceptable drinking establishment is born.

It isn't busy in here. There's just me, the bartender, two old guys watching sports highlights on the TV behind the bar, and a guy in a Leafs toque shooting pool by himself.

I want to order a gin and tonic, but I'm worried I'll be judged. This is rum country. Rye for special occasions. I ask for a rum and Coke and let the bartender know to keep them coming, which is unnecessary; drinking with purpose is the Pennington default. The old men, one hidden behind a bushy beard, the other behind a swollen red nose, look me over with mild curiosity. I offer a stiff, deliberate nod. They aren't impressed and turn their attention back to the TV. Fair enough. I am, if nothing else, unimpressive.

During the first drink, the glass shakes in my hand.

During the second, I'm able to relax my neck and shoulders, tense from driving and stress and twenty-eight years of bad posture.

During the third drink, I take stock of my situation. Everything I own is wedged into the back of my 1993 Dodge Ramcharger sitting outside the Goode Night Inn. I haven't showered in three days because I've been driving and sleeping in the truck. My brown hair is dark with grease and pressed flat under a frayed Flames ball cap. I haven't changed my clothes since leaving Calgary because, with a stunning lack of foresight, I buried them in a suitcase under a large flat-screen TV, a pretty decent stereo, one box of books, two boxes of CDs, and two miscellaneous boxes marked "STUFF," and couldn't be bothered to dig them out along the way. Now I'm drinking in Pennington, Nova Scotia, the place I was raised and the place I left without fanfare as soon as I could. My bank account is worth about $300 and my credit card, now being charged $49 a night by the Goode family, has limited runway. I think that's about it.

During the fourth drink, I wallow in a deep and profound melancholy, questioning every choice I've ever made and throwing blame anywhere I think it might stick.

On the fifth drink, I am recognized.

"Macallister?"

Shit.

"Hey, Macallister!"

Turning on my stool, I meet the eyes that belong to the head that belongs to the pool-playing Leafs toque.

Paulie Coleman. He's older and quite a bit heavier, but it's definitely him.

"Paul. Paulie. Hi," I say, without smiling.

"Hey, man. Wow. Adam fucking Macallister. Long time," he says with enough smile for both of us.

I haven't thought about Paulie in a decade, but suddenly remember everything about him. Nice guy, kind of dim, enthusiastic without discrimination. He has apple cheeks and everything he says is too loud by half. When we played peewee hockey, he took a wild swing at a flying puck and clipped a kid on the other team. The kid went down like, well, like someone had just tried to decapitate him with a hockey stick. Paulie got suspended for six games, though if you asked him, it was a bullshit call. "I was going for the puck," he'd cried. "How is that against the rules?" He didn't make a lot of time for nuance.

"Yeah, it's been a while," I say.

"Yeah, man, like forever." He rubs his forehead with his wrist, pushing his toque askew. "So, what have you been up to?"

It's a vague and open-ended question, considering he hasn't seen me in ten years. If anyone else had asked it, I'd assume they were making polite conversation. But Paulie oozes earnestness. He's genuinely curious and, for reasons that have more to do with the rum than a burning desire to play catch-up, we grab some stools overlooking the ice and we talk. We talk and we drink. We drink a lot, actually, and the more I drink, the more I offer details of my life—a careful selection of the places I've been and things I've done that might impress a guy like Paulie. I dial everything up about thirty percent because why the hell not, and when I get to the part about being a sports reporter in Calgary, I build myself up like I'm the second coming of Ring Lardner.

"And you're just here for a visit?" he asks, nonplussed by everything I've just said.

"I guess I'm sort of working. I'm only here for a week, but it's not a vacation or anything." This is sort of true.

"Oh yeah? What do you mean?" he asks.

"It's just this thing I'm writing about my dad." Not strictly untrue. "It's a feature for *Sports Illustrated*." Now I'm mostly lying. "You know, the way he played hockey and how people remember him, but really it's about how hockey's violent culture fits into today's society." I made that part up just now. "And it's about redemption." Oh god, stop talking already.

"What about you," I ask, trying to shift the onus onto him. "What have you been up to?"

"Oh, you know, nothing really," he says, scratching the inside of his ear with his pinky finger. "Just caught in the comfort zone. I do some roadwork in the summer, get my pogey in the winter. Live lean when it runs out." He's still living with his parents, a fact he offers without excuse or embarrassment. It's the simple truth of Paulie.

The game on the ice below us ends with a long whistle from the referee, and the players—men between thirty and sixty years old, senior leaguers who have been playing against each other in various combinations for decades— make their way off. A couple stay behind shooting pucks into the empty net, squeezing in a few more minutes of ice time.

And then I see him. My father. He's pulling the large doors at the far end of the ice and propping them open, before disappearing back into the Zamboni room. He doesn't look up because he has no idea I'm only two hundred feet away.

"I didn't think he'd be here this late," I say.

Paulie squints at the ice to see what I'm looking at. "Your

old man? He's always here. I assumed you were staying next door with him."

"Next door? Dad's not on Duke Street anymore?" Are there even houses next door to the rink? There didn't used to be.

"He's just down the hall there," Paulie says, gesturing toward the door.

"Down the hall?"

"Yeah, man." Paulie looks at the door quizzically, taking a second to confirm this fact to himself. "Like ten feet down the hall," he says, as though it was the details of the hall itself eluding me.

Below us, the Zamboni pulls out onto the ice, my father at the wheel.

"When did that happen?"

"I dunno, a few years ago. You said all that stuff about *Sports Illustrated* or whatever, I figured you'd talked to him."

"No," I say, trying to remember when I last spoke to my father on the phone. A few years ago, probably on my birthday or Christmas or something, seems about right. "Not yet."

"Last call, guys," the bartender calls out behind us. I've never needed another drink so much.

·

Terrance James Macallister was born on a farm just outside Pennington in 1947, the son of sheep farmer Ellis Macallister and his wife, Agnes.

Terry learned to skate on a pond behind the barn when he was five years old, but didn't start playing organized hockey until he was thirteen. The years of pond skating and farm chores paid off and Terry became a local star overnight, powering through the other kids and scoring almost at will. To compensate, they made him play with the older children, and at just fifteen he joined the Pennington Royals, a junior team of seventeen- and eighteen-year-olds. He scored fifty-four goals, a record at the time.

After Terry had been with the Royals for a year, a man showed up at the farm and offered him a chance to play for the Toronto Marlboros in the Ontario Hockey Association. Terry wasn't as successful against the bigger, faster, and more skilled players in the OHA, but he worked hard and carved out a role, using his farm-boy strength to beat up players whenever his coach asked him to, which ended up being fairly often. Beating people up on the ice would become Terry's calling in life, and his ability to intimidate pretty much everyone else in the league helped the Marlies win a lot of hockey games. Over a three-game stretch in the playoffs during his first year with the team, Terry had three different one-punch knockouts, and while records aren't kept on such things, no one could remember seeing anything like it before. A reporter for the *Toronto Telegram* dubbed him Terry Punchout and the name stuck.

Terry wasn't drafted by an NHL team, but he got an invitation to the Toronto Maple Leafs training camp when he was nineteen. During his first scrimmage, he beat the holy hell out of the Leafs' long-standing tough guy, George "Duck" Wilkins, making a good impression on all the people on whom you want to make good impressions. A week later, Duck was traded to St. Louis and, on October 14, 1967, Terry Punchout made his professional hockey debut. He would go on to play 1,032 regular season games over the next fifteen years. He scored 119 goals and added 301 assists. By any statistical standard, it was a bad hockey career, but Terry also accumulated 3,994 penalty minutes, more than any player before or since. It's a dubious record, not the sort of thing that would put him in the Hall of Fame, but it made him a legend, nonetheless. There isn't a hockey fan alive who doesn't know his name. His hometown named a stadium after him.

I know all this about Terry Punchout because I know everything about Terry Punchout. I have every stat and every milestone memorized, and I know a few things that aren't in the record books. His favourite colour is green. He's allergic to rabbits. He likes to drink rum and Coke in a tall glass with lots of ice.

What I didn't know is that he now lives in the same rink they named after him, the same rink where he's been driving the Zamboni since I was fifteen years old.

I need to piss so bad it hurts, but I'm afraid to open my eyes. The problem with rum is the hangover. It isn't like other hangovers; it gets inside every part of you. I can feel it in my hair. Paulie and I had already had more than enough to drink when the bartender shut us down. Still, we convinced him to sell us a bottle of dark rum for sixty bucks, which I'm fairly sure came from my wallet, and we opened it in the parking lot.

I lift my eyelid just a sliver and blinding, unimaginable light pours into my skull. My stomach lurches. It takes several hard blinks for the room around me to slowly take shape. Flowery wallpaper. Bay windows. Fake plants. I'm on a large grey couch with thick, soft cushions, my long body stiff from bending while I slept. On the coffee table in front of the couch is a tall glass of water resting on a small white doily. Beside the glass is a bottle of Extra Strength Tylenol. Beside that is a bowl of potpourri. The rich, lavender scent only makes me feel worse. I take a deep breath and lift myself up on my left side, nice and slow. The childproof cap on the pill bottle is a struggle, but I manage to spill four tablets into my hand. I try to choke them dry for fear of adding more water to my already taxed bladder, but there's not enough spit and the pills turn into a bitter paste on my tongue. I gag a little and grab the glass. A sip turns into a mouthful. The water is tepid, but I'm a sponge, and empty it in three swallows. I figure I've got about two minutes to find a toilet.

Steeling myself, I stand in one jerky motion. The room tilts impossibly, and while the rational part of me under-stands this is the hangover challenging my senses, there is another part of me that is surprised furniture isn't crashing into the wall. I take a beat to let the room level itself, which is when I notice I'm not wearing clothes.

It is at this precise moment, leaning hard to my right in just my boxer shorts, that my grade-school music teacher walks into the room.

"Oh, good, you're up," she says, ignoring nearly everything that's happening in front of her. "I just woke Paul for breakfast. I hope you don't mind, but I threw your clothes in the wash with his. They seemed a bit grubby. Are you hungry?"

There are a lot of things I want to do right now—cover myself up, apologize profusely, throw up, die a quick death—but there is one very pressing matter to deal with first.

"Can I use your washroom?"

"Sure," she says, "it's upstairs. The one with the toilet."

While pissing, I remember making Paulie sit and drink with me on a concrete slab in the rec centre parking lot so I could see my father again, though I didn't say that out loud. And sure enough, after about thirty minutes—after the beer-league players and old guys from the bar and even the bartender had cleared out—my father came to the front door to lock up the building. He did it from the inside, then disappeared back into the darkness of the lobby like Pennington's Quasimodo. It was hard enough coming back here knowing I needed something from him, that I needed him. I'd promised myself I'd get through this without changing my feelings toward him—a contrived mix of anger and ambivalence. But now I just feel sorry for him.

·

After relieving myself and putting on Paulie's too-big sweat-pants and too-bigger sweatshirt, I enter the Coleman dining room. Mrs. Coleman is setting a stack of pancakes on the table, while Paulie, who doesn't look like he's suffering nearly as much as I am, piles bacon onto his plate. Mr. Coleman reads the local paper, the *Pennington Weekly Record*. Taking in the spread, I can understand why Paulie is comfortable living at home. Pancakes, scrambled eggs, bacon, juice, and coffee on a weekday morning. I can only assume Mrs. Coleman retired from teaching music and has now gone insane caring for her husband and only son. She looks about the same as she did back in Grade 4: tiny, with sharp blue eyes behind large, gold-rimmed glasses. Her hair has more silver in it and she appears to have shrunk a good foot and a half, though that probably has more to do with me not being eight years old anymore. I sit and nod as she offers me coffee.

"So how have you been using your time, Mr. Macallister?" She called everyone in her classes Mr. and Miss. Back then it seemed respectful, but now it feels silly.

"Um." I take a gulp from my coffee to stall and burn my tongue.

"He's been living in Calgary," Paulie offers.

"Oh, that's nice," says Mrs. Coleman. "Charlie and I went to the Stampede back in 1976 and had a wonderful time. And you're just home for a visit?"

"He's writing a thing about Punch for *Sports Illustrated*," Paulie says.

Jesus, I told him that, didn't I?

"Really?" asks Mr. Coleman, looking up over his newspaper. "And how is your father?"

Mr. Coleman once threw a cassette tape of mine out the window of a moving vehicle. I made the tape to play in the dressing room before games and filled it with singalong stadium rock and obscene rap classics. Paulie borrowed it to make a copy, and stuck it in the tape deck of his dad's minivan on the way home. Mr. Coleman is a reserved guy, level-headed on all matters of music and politics, so when 2 Live Crew's "Fuck Martinez"—a profanity-filled song targeting a Florida politician who had tried to have the group's earlier profanity-filled songs banned—came on, he didn't approve. The song played for about half a minute before Mr. Coleman hit eject, casually rolled down his window, and fired it out into the night.

"He's good, I guess," I say, and chew on a piece of bacon. My tongue appreciates the salt, but my stomach is still unsure.

"I can't even think of the last time I saw him," Mr. Coleman says. "To be honest, I didn't realize he was still around." When he says "around," he means "alive," because he is now, as ever, an asshole.

"Oh, I see him puttering around down at the rink sometimes," Mrs. Coleman says, smiling. "He looks well."

"Maybe I just haven't been paying attention," says Mr. Coleman. "So, what does *Sports Illustrated* want with old Terry Punchout, anyway?"

It's a fair question—it's been a long time since anyone gave a shit about my father—but there's something in his tone that bugs me. Old Terry Punchout? Mr. Coleman and my father are about the same age.

"Bobby Monaghan will break Dad's penalty record this year, so he's relevant right now," I say. "People are talking about him and he's been off the grid so long they want to know what he's been up to. Hockey stars don't usually disappear like he did." I'm overselling again. Especially when it's entirely possible my father will want nothing to do with any of this.

"Well, hockey stars might not disappear," Mr. Coleman says with a laugh, "but he wasn't exactly Bobby Orr." He lifts his paper back up between us again, but keeps talking through it. "I can't imagine a lot of people are looking for Zamboni-driving tips."

It's not that he's dismissive of my father that bothers me, it's that he's dismissive of my story. When I first pitched a piece about my dad a few months ago, it was in a Vancouver bar and I was drunk enough to do it with conviction. Now that it's a thing I actually need to write—a thing my livelihood depends on—I have my doubts, and this guy isn't helping.

"I think his rookie card is worth about a hundred bucks," Paulie mumbles through a mouthful of pancake. "You know, if the corners are sharp. That's pretty good."

We all look at him for a few seconds, but no one responds. It's Mrs. Coleman who finally breaks the silence by saying, "Oh, Charlie." She smiles at me and waves her hand dismissively at her husband. "Don't listen to him. This all sounds very impressive, Adam. Good for you. Your father must be excited."

Mr. Coleman glances over the top of his paper at his wife and something in her eyes cows him. "Well, it's been a few years since I've read *Sports Illustrated*. Maybe I'll give it a skim if Terry's on the cover."

Paulie stabs at the stack of pancakes and pulls another two onto his plate, and I turn my attention to my own food.

A lot of people in Pennington love my father, or at least they love the idea of him, but it's not universal. When I was nine, he was described in the *Weekly Record* as a "violent reprobate" by J.J. Johnstone, another local hero. About the same time my father was starting out in the NHL, J.J. left Pennington to take theology classes at St. Francis Xavier in

Antigonish, intent on becoming a priest. He came back to town one year short of graduating and took a job reporting for the paper. A year later, he took over for the retiring sports editor and has run the paper's sports pages ever since, and I assume he still does.

J.J. never liked my father. While Dad was making his name in the pros, the *Weekly Record* shared surprisingly little about him. Then, when my father retired in 1982, J.J. wrote a long treatise about how the end of Dad's career gave the league a chance to clean up its act and get back to what J.J. called "pure hockey," not the "goony sideshow hockey played by the likes of Terry Punchout." I didn't know any of this stuff at the time. In 1984, the town built a new rec centre and decided to name the arena after somebody. The two names put forward were the ex-pro hockey player and the long-time sports editor. Town council voted 7–0 in favour of Macallister Stadium (that the new bar is called J.J.'s is probably a consolation prize), prompting the "violent reprobate" comment and a long conversation between my mother and me about why J.J. was so mean to my dad. The cruel irony of asking her, the one person with good reason to hate my father, didn't occur to me until much, much later. That she defended him in that moment is as good an example of the kind of person she was that you'll ever find.

•

After breakfast, Paulie drives me back to the motel. I'm still wearing his clothes, which hang loose on my body.

"Hey, wanna watch the Leafs game tonight? Have some beers? We'll be at Mac's place. I can pick you up."

To my surprise, I want to go. Whatever apprehension I had last night about being seen seems to be gone. Hanging out with guys from high school might be fun. I'm not even sure who's still around.

"Yeah, sure," I say.

"Cool, man. I'll come get you around six."

"Alright." I open the door and step out. "Oh, thanks for letting me crash. And for the clothes."

"No worries." I slam the car door shut and Paulie flashes a peace sign as he pulls away, leaving me in the parking lot next to my truck. I should have asked for his help to dig out my clothes. There's a slow, thick, and slushy rainfall, and moving my TV and stereo and boxes without getting them wet is a two-man job. But showing him that all my worldly possessions are packed up back there doesn't really jibe with the image I'm trying to project.

After a quick shower to wash off last night's stink, I put Paulie's sweats back on and make a trip to the mall. The drive is my first daylight look at Pennington. MacDonell Books, Pat's Pub, Cathy's Flower Shoppe, Clovie's Diner, and so on; a few things are missing and there are new additions. It's like seeing a photo of myself from a day I don't remember. But it feels the same. That's the problem with home: even if I hate it, it's still home. We're wired for familiarity. It's a design flaw.

Turning left onto Elm Street, I come to the first significant change in landscape. Not only has the Capitol Theatre closed, but the building is also gone, leaving a vacant lot. It's not even paved, just empty space with a few years of unchecked growth and a tilted "For Sale" sign jammed into a mound of dirt, its colours faded by the sun.

The Capitol Theatre was one of Pennington's top teenager hot spots. It was where I saw *Return of the Jedi* and *Back to the Future* and *Terminator 2*. My first date (Amanda Gallant, *Aladdin*) happened there. Actually, my first twenty or so dates happened there. My first kiss with tongue (Karen Yeo, *Groundhog Day*), my first hickey (Sabrina Turner, *Mrs. Doubtfire*), and my first honest-to-God boob grab (Danielle Morrison, under the shirt but over the bra, *True Lies*) all happened in the darkness of the Capitol. How the hell are kids learning about sex now?

The mall parking lot is mostly empty. The Mayfair Mall isn't big, anchored by the town's liquor store at one end and an IGA at the other. The Frenchy's Thrift Shop I'm looking for is still there, and after some digging I find a pair of jeans my size and a couple of T-shirts, including a vintage Nordiques shirt that's kind of cool, the sort of thing I might wear even if I wasn't desperate. Taking my finds to the register, I'm stupefied when I come face to face with Stephanie Smith.

Our high school didn't officially have a prom queen— proms were cancelled in the early nineties because most kids preferred to head into the woods to drink beer and set pallets we'd steal from behind the mall on fire—but if we'd had one, it would have been Stephanie Smith. She was beautiful, and from Grade 9 on she rarely acknowledged my existence. My above-average acne and below-average self-esteem placed me firmly in Sir John Thompson High School's middle class, well outside the scope of anything Stephanie gave a shit about.

The horrible high school girl who wields power over all the popular kids and makes life miserable for the un-popular ones might be a cliché, but Stephanie embraced it. When Tamara Cormier got her period and bled through a pair of white pants, it was Stephanie who started calling her Tamara Tampon and it was Stephanie who kept call-ing her Tamara Tampon long after everyone else stopped thinking it was funny, which it never really was. There was a rumour that Tamara tried to commit suicide by eating a handful of pills. The pills, however, were Extra Strength Advil and only caused a mild gastric bleed. Even after that story made the rounds, Stephanie didn't stop with the Tamara Tampon stuff. She was a terror to the social proletariat, and I probably got off lucky just falling into the category of people she ignored.

But all of that was from another lifetime, a million years ago. Now Stephanie Smith is the girl selling used clothes at Frenchy's. She's still beautiful, even though she's wearing too much makeup, giving her skin a salmon hue. Her black blouse cuts low, drawing attention to her cleavage, as spectacular now as it was when she first started showing it off in junior high.

Holy shit, it's Stephanie Smith!

"Hi." Now, you'd think I'd be bothered by how awful this girl was, but I'm not. I only think of the gorgeous, popular Stephanie I fantasized about as a teenager. My heart is racing, which I know is ridiculous, and feeling ridiculous only makes me more nervous.

She offers a curt smile, and there's an awkward pause as we eye each other, waiting for someone to initiate the transaction. Stephanie isn't wearing a wedding ring, and I imagine a thousand scenarios for why she'd be single, most of them involving fate pushing us toward several days of amazing sex in my room at the Goode Night Inn. At this moment, I can think of no greater victory in life than finally sleeping with all the girls who have so thoroughly rejected me over the years.

"Can I help you?"

Help me? You have no idea.

"Um, no." More awkward staring. "I'd like to buy these." I thrust the clothes at her. "It's me. Adam. Macallister. From high school." I have never been less cool.

Stephanie nods and purses her lips. "Mm-hmm." She takes the clothes and punches some buttons on the cash register. "Eighteen dollars." She looks through me and I understand I'm getting the cold shoulder from Stephanie Smith. How is this possible? She works at Frenchy's! I (almost) write for *Sports Illustrated*! I live in Calgary! I am a fully formed, successful adult! Or, at least as far as she knows (sweatpants aside), I am. Are social hierarchies, like the Ten Commandments, carved in stone and inalterable forever? Stephanie Smith is selling me a pair of used jeans and all the rules of high school somehow still apply. Well, fuck you, lady!

I don't actually say this to her. I give her a twenty, accept my change, and shrink into a fog of doubt and self-loathing. All it took was her aloof stare and I'm broken. A few minutes later, sitting in my truck in the parking lot, I am incredulous about what has just happened, and it would be really nice to have someone around to laugh about it with.

•

After I change my clothes, I stop at a gas station to fill up the Dodge. I check the oil and the tire pressure. These aren't pressing issues, but I excel at procrastinating. If I knew how to check spark plugs or whatever a manifold is, I'd do it. As it is, my knowledge of cars is limited, and after about ten minutes, I'm out of things to examine. And not just with the Ramcharger, but anywhere. I've killed as much day as I can, and it's time to do the thing I came here to do.

The door to my father's apartment is unexceptional. There's no number or sign or peephole, nothing to indicate a human being lives behind it. It could be a broom closet. If

Paulie hadn't called it to my attention, the door would have gone unnoticed by me, as it likely is by everybody. It is a door that may as well not exist. I knock on it.

I hear the creak of a chair, some shuffling footsteps, and a few unintelligible grunts. Then, sure enough, my father opens the door. I don't speak and he doesn't speak. We just stand there, not speaking. I wasn't sure how I'd feel, seeing him. I thought I'd convinced myself I didn't care, but now that I'm here I want to hug him. And punch him in the face. At the same time.

He's only fifty-eight, but he looks so much older. His back is hunched and his hair is white and stringy, sticking out in all directions from under an old black-and-red newsboy cap. He's wearing a cotton union suit, the top half exposed and stained with sweat, the bottom covered by saggy dark work pants held up with suspenders. I've been taller than my father since I was fourteen, but now he looks small, weak and worn and wizened. His face is in ruins. His bum right hand hangs limp at his side. Fifty-eight? Shit, he could be ninety. He could be a thousand.

"Dad, it's me. It's Adam." It's the second time today I've felt the need to identify myself to someone I know.

He stays quiet. He doesn't offer a hug or a handshake or a smile. Just bewildered silence.

"Can I come in?" When I imagined this moment, I wasn't the one driving the conversation. I'd show up, and he'd offer a lifetime of apologies without excuses. Not that I'd forgive him so quick, but he'd work hard at it and make me understand, or at least accept, how we got here, and then a day would come when we looked back at the ten years I'd been gone, we'd shake our heads as if to say, *Wow, we really mucked that up. Good thing we're sorted now.* No part of me actually believed that's how it would go, but if you're fantasizing about a significant life event, why wouldn't you make it happy?

My father steps out of the doorway so I can enter. His apartment is a concrete box, a prison cell with few creature comforts. The walls are grey and bare. A card table holds a hot plate. He has a small fridge, the kind I used to keep beer in as a university student. In the centre of the room is a green recliner, the fabric torn on the right arm. It's pointed at one of those big old console TVs resting on the floor, more furniture than appliance. There are dirty dishes piled on top of it. A sagging cot sits against another wall. No windows, no plants, no pictures. The lights are fluorescent. Forcing someone to live in this room would surely violate an international human rights treaty.

My father closes the door. He looks at me, then he looks around the room that is, it seems, his home. He grinds his teeth, mouth tight. He looks like he's trying to eat a potato chip without anyone hearing it crunch. The TV flickers with CBC's five o'clock news, the picture tinged pink and riddled with static.

"How are you?" I ask. He jumps, just a little, as though my voice frightens him.

"Adam. I didn't know..." he trails off. Then, with firmness, he says, "You should have called," and gathers the dishes on the TV. He sets them in the deep, square sink next to his mini-fridge. Above the sink there's a small shelf holding a bottle of dish soap and a tube of toothpaste. As far as I can tell, there's no phone in here. What exactly does he think I should have called him on?

"Yeah. Sorry, you're right. I should have called. I lost your number, I guess. It's been a while, you know?" Of course he knows. He keeps tidying as best he can, but there's a lot of clutter—shoes, dirty clothes, newspapers—and nowhere to put any of it. He ends up just pushing the mess around the room. Finally, he faces me.

"Are you hungry? I'm hungry. We can go down to the canteen and get some fries." Now he's looking past me, at the door.

"Why don't we go out and get something?" I ask.

"Oh, I can't go anywhere. I'll need to clean the ice shortly."

"Okay, is the bar open? J.J.'s? We can get a drink."

"I don't drink."

"Since when? You know, it doesn't matter. Canteen fries would be great."

"Okay, fries," he says, picking up a coat from the end of the cot and herding me toward the door with it. "And some hot chocolate."

Right. And some hot chocolate.

•

In the stadium, a dozen or so parents sit behind the benches on either side of the ice, cheering on a group of kids who look to be about six or seven years old. The goalies are ludicrous in their giant pads, standing bored for long stretches of time as their teammates try to swat the puck up and down the ice. It's cute, sure, but not action-packed—though you wouldn't know it listening to the screaming adults. Hockey parents are invested. They spend an unreasonable amount of time dragging their kids to and from rinks. The kids develop lifelong rivalries with other kids from other towns—they play and win and lose and fight with each other for years. And after each game, their parents reward them with pizza and pop. It conditions them to think that beating those kids from those towns is good. Then they grow up and have their own children and the cycle repeats itself. Winning, losing, fighting. Pizza and pop. And parents in the stands yelling at players, referees, each other, and so on, shitheads begetting shitheads for all of time.

My father and I sit near the corner, quietly watching the game with our french fries and hot chocolates. The Pennington Rec Centre canteen specializes in soggy fries drowned in lumpy beef gravy and thin, generic ketchup. I'm not complaining. I grew up on this potato slurry. This is comfort food.

"So how long have you been living up there?" These are the first words either one of us has spoken since we sat down.

"Awhile."

"You should have told me." What I'd have done with the information, I don't know.

"Not much to tell. You don't tell me when you move." Which is true, I don't. I'm not even sure he knows I was living in Calgary. We've spoken on the phone a handful of times over the years, but the calls were always short, pointless, and fewer and further between as time went on. "It's not like you send me Christmas cards," he says.

"Mail goes both ways, Dad." Neither one of us is scoring points here. This a pissing contest between men dealing with their own hurt feelings.

On the ice, one kid manages a breakaway and stutter-steps his way toward the goal. When he gets about five feet from the goalie, he comes to a full stop, winds up, and swings at the puck with everything he has, missing completely and crashing to the ice. The rest of the kids catch up and they all tumble over each other like bowling pins. Next to me, my father slurps his hot chocolate.

"*Sports Illustrated* wants to do a story about you. They want me to write it." I throw it out there. It won't make things more awkward, that's for sure.

"Why would they want to do that?"

How come every time I mention this article to people, they don't immediately recognize how great of an idea it is?

"You're famous, Dad. Well, infamous, I guess. And you've been hiding out for a long time. People want to know what happened to you."

"And what happened to me?" he asks, more to himself than me, so I don't answer. "Nobody cares what happened to me."

"Well, *Sports Illustrated* cares," I say, trying my best to sound enthusiastic. "That's the entire reason I'm here. You should be excited. You should be flattered."

"I coulda saved you the trip. Tell them thanks but no thanks."

"Dad, this is a big deal." The parents behind the bench farthest from us erupt as one of the kids shovels the puck over the goal line.

"It's not something I'm interested in." He puts his Styrofoam cup down and rubs the jagged pink scar on the back of his right hand like he's hoping to buff out the damage.

"It's *Sports Illustrated*. It's the biggest deal."

"Not to me. Thank you—really, thank you—but no."

I had considered this possibility. It's another reason I didn't reach out before I came—I figured it'd be harder to turn me down to my face, and if he did, I could use any guilt he might have against him to change his mind. "Dad, this is a big deal to me. I need this. I need you to do this for me. Please." I hate myself for begging and I hate him for making me do it. "Dad, you owe me this."

"What do I owe you?"

I have no idea what he owes me. "It's just a couple of interviews. We'll go somewhere and you talk into a tape recorder. Just tell some stories and I'll ask a few questions. That's it. You don't have to do anything. Just give me some details and then you can go back to hiding."

My father swirls his hot chocolate.

"I've never asked you for anything before." I feel like a kid trying to negotiate his way into staying up late.

He sighs. "Just do something else. Find someone else. This can't be that important."

"On a scale of one to ten, this is like a forty-two. I wouldn't be here if it wasn't."

"You wouldn't be here," he repeats back quietly, staring into the dark, chocolatey sludge at the bottom of his cup. "Just talking? No taking my picture or anything?"

"No pictures. They'll use old photos from when you played. So you'll do it?"

"We'll have to do it here."

"Actually, it's a bit echoey in here. It'll be better for the recording if we go somewhere else."

"I don't have time to be running around town telling stories. We can do it up in my room."

"Yeah, sure. Whatever gets it done."

The buzzer signals the end of the game, and the kids swarm from the benches onto the ice to shake hands. They have to do this. It's supposed to promote sportsmanship. The parents on both sides are clapping, though there's a discernible lack of enthusiasm on the losing side.

"I need to clean the ice. Come back tomorrow. We'll see how it goes."

"Alright, tomorrow. Sounds good." I exhale and it feels like I've spent my life holding my breath. Maybe this will work out for me, after all. I've read a thousand athlete profiles and a lot of players like to talk about how they bet on themselves. It's a stupid cliché because stupid clichés are the first language of all athletes, but I've never actually tried betting on myself to do something difficult, and now that I am—admittedly, more out of necessity than anything else—I'm suddenly surging with something that feels dangerously close to self-confidence. It's intoxicating. I want to stay focused, step up, dig deep, give it a hundred and ten percent, play the game the right way, and do what it takes to win.

My father descends the stairs and heads toward the Zamboni room. "Thanks," I call after him, because there's no "I" in "team," but he doesn't respond. I tell myself that it's a marathon, not a sprint.

•

I was born in New York, but don't remember ever living there. Before I was two years old, my parents split up and my mother brought me back to Pennington, while my father went off to Los Angeles to play for the Kings. For the first couple of years, we lived with my mom's parents. I sort of remember that—flashes of my grandfather playing solitaire on a TV tray and the taste of my grandmother's maple fudge.

By the time I was five, my mother worked at the hospital delivering meals to patients and we'd moved into a small apartment on Jasper Street. Most of the other apartments were occupied by widows and spinsters who'd take turns babysitting me. The only other kid in the place was Dave Arsenault.

Dave and I were the same age, both the sons of single mothers. People like to think they pick their friends. You believe they are the people you want—people who complement you, people you want in your life. Maybe that's true sometimes, but usually it's just proximity and circumstance. Back then, if I'd thought up the criteria for an ideal best friend, it's improbable the best match would have been the kid downstairs. But Dave and I became best friends precisely because he was the kid downstairs.

We weren't allowed to leave the immediate neighbourhood, but both our mothers worked, so it was an impossible rule to enforce. Most days, we'd sneak off to the Duck Pond, which was our Neverland. It was tucked away beside a small wood, surrounded by marsh and reeds, and fed by a deep, narrow stream. We called it the Duck Pond because it was a pond and there were sometimes ducks and we weren't wildly creative. There was a fort in the trees built by the kids who came before us and left for the kids who came after. To get to the fort, you had to shimmy over a plank that crossed the stream, then climb rotting boards nailed into the side of a tree. In retrospect, I'm surprised there were no accidents, drownings or deaths.

We made it a rule that to use the fort, you had to help stock it with supplies. I delivered an empty Quality Street tin for storage purposes. Dave provided a box of wooden matches. One kid added an FM shower radio, another a milk crate we used as a table, and another brought a deck of cards minus the four of spades and both red queens. We collected a hammer and some nails for basic repairs, and kept two cans of beans in case someone had to "crash," which was just wishful thinking. But it was Paulie who brought us the most valuable item of all: a small stack of vintage *Playboy* and *Penthouse* magazines pinched from his father.

"What if he knows you took them?" I asked, because I was the sort of kid who was too afraid of getting caught to enjoy being bad. More than once I've been accused of hating fun.

"He won't. He has boxes of them." Paulie would later

prove this to us at a sleepover. Even by today's standards, with infinite access to internet pornography, Mr. Coleman had a collection of staggering size and scope.

We were grateful to Paulie for introducing us to naked women. We'd read *Penthouse Forum* for laughs, with no understanding of what it was we were laughing at. Our comprehension of erotic stories was only slightly better than our comprehension of quantum physics.

The Duck Pond was also where Dave and I tried our first cigarettes, which he stole from his mother's purse. The menthol 100s were comically long in our small mouths, more like straws than smokes. He struck his match on the first try and sucked the flame into the tip of the cigarette. It was easily the coolest thing I'd ever seen.

"You just suck it in. Like breathing," Dave said, handing it to me.

I didn't get the difference between pulling the smoke into my mouth and pulling it into my lungs. I not only inhaled, I inhaled with gusto, mentholated smoke scratching my throat and burning my chest. I coughed the lit cigarette into my lap, then panicked, slapping it away before it singed my pants. I tried again, trying to get the smoke in and out smoothly, until I was overcome with dizziness and vomited down the fort's trap door onto every step of the ladder we needed to climb down. Dave made fun of me for months.

The day of the cigarette incident I came home and both my mother and my father were in the living room. After he retired from playing, Dad moved back to Toronto and I'd only see him once or twice a year, when he'd blow into town for a few days, ostensibly to visit me, but also for a dose of hero worship. People in Pennington still loved him and would throw a town barbecue or a party at the curling club for his visits. I looked up to him, my dad the NHL star. Other kids were jealous; they had fisherman and truck driver and accountant dads. Every kid thinks his dad is a superhero, but mine kind of was.

As I walked into our living room, my father grinned at me from the beat-up rocking chair in the corner. His hair was still dark then, almost black, and he wore a mustard-coloured sweater. My mother, sitting on the couch, stared out the window, keeping her eyes turned away from him.

"Hey, Skinny," my father said. He always called me Skinny, not Champ or Tiger or Kiddo. Skinny. Which I was, but still.

I wanted to run over and jump into his arms, but I could tell something was off. My mother was the kind of angry you can feel in the air and I wasn't sure if it was me or my father that was pissing her off.

"Come here and give me a hug," he said, sliding to the edge of the chair. I glanced at my mother, unsure, then slowly walked over and hugged my father. His arms wrapped around me and his hair, stiff with lanolin, felt like twigs against my cheek. "I've got some news. Good news. I'm moving here."

My mother's face shot to us, her eyes wide and fiery in a way I'd never seen.

"Oh, well, not here," he said, gesturing to the small room we were sitting in. "Into town, a house over on Duke Street. You can come stay whenever you want."

I was ecstatic. Who wouldn't have been? My father was coming home!

That night, when mom put me to bed, I asked her why she was mad. I wasn't under any illusions that my parents would get back together, but it seemed unfair of her to not want him around, especially since I wanted it so much.

"It's hard to explain," she said, pulling my blanket up a

little higher on my chest, then smoothing it out with her palm. My mother rarely spoke about my father. She never interfered with the relationship he and I had, limited as it was. She made sure there was a framed photo of him in my room, but she didn't talk about him when he wasn't around.

"Do you hate Dad?"

I was so afraid she'd say yes. I loved my father and wanted him to live here, but I was loyal to her first. If she really hated him, I'd have to take her side.

"I get mad at him. Sometimes I get very mad at him, but it's not the same thing as hate. It can be hard to tell the difference."

"Can't you pretend to not be mad at him? Not all the time, just when you see him." This seemed reasonable, in the way her asking me to pretend I was okay eating broccoli at my grandparents' house was reasonable. Sometimes you just have to suck it up, right? She looked at me, smiling a little with her mouth, but not her eyes. They were sad as ever.

"I'll try." She leaned over and kissed me on my forehead.

As she turned the light off and walked out the door, I asked her the one question I'd been thinking about since the moment my father told me he was coming home.

"Do you think Dad will coach my hockey team next year?"

She stopped in the doorway but didn't turn back. "Maybe. You'll have to ask him. Now go to sleep."

•

I'm sitting in a basement with a bunch of guys I grew up with: Paulie, Shitty, Mac, and Davey Arsehole. To them, I am just Macallister. None of these are the names our mothers gave us, but in our mothers' defence, they didn't know us very well when we were born.

Paulie is Paulie because Paul always seemed too stiff and adult. He isn't apostle material, or even Beatle material for that matter.

Shitty is Jason MacDonald—the most common first-and-last-name combination among men aged twenty-five to thirty in Pennington. Of the four I grew up with, there's Jay Corn Flakes, also known as Flakes, Flakey, or Flaker; Lefty, a left-handed goalie, which is only slightly more common than a unicorn in a small town where left-handed gear is hard to come by; Jason de Toof, named for his strange accent, an odd mix of Acadian father, Cape Breton mother, and harelip; and Shitty. Shitty's dad, Doug MacDonald, got dubbed Dougie Two-Shits in his youth because of his propensity for one-upmanship. If you took one shit, good old Dougie would tell you about the time he shit twice. As Dougie Two-Shits's son, Jason was called Shit Stain as early as in the womb. By the time he was twelve, Shit Stain had morphed into Shitty—a nickname for a nickname—to everyone except his teachers, who would often call on "Jason" and get no response. Going through life being called Shitty by an entire town has to mess you up at least a little.

Mac is Clint MacLean. I wish I'd been called Mac, though half the people in Pennington are McThis or MacThat and probably feel the same. Clint's dad was an absolute giant of a man, appropriately called Big Mac. Though Clint did inherit his father's size and thick mop of curls, he was Little Mac until the age of ten. That's when Big Mac drowned in the St. Lawrence. After that, people stopped distinguishing and he was just Mac.

Davey Arsehole is David Arsenault, my former downstairs neighbour and best friend. I always just called him Dave.

Mine is a lazy nickname. I am Macallister, no bells or

whistles or superfluous hard "E" sounds. It's better than nothing. The kids who don't play hockey don't get nicknames; they're just Steven or Peter or Michael. The nicknames cut in dressing rooms bleed into the rest of our lives. For all the romanticizing of hockey in this country, no one ever mentions that, in places like Pennington, it's literally responsible for your identity.

Mac looks like Paul Bunyan, big as ever, wearing a bushy beard and a red flannel shirt. He inherited this house from his dead father by way of his uncle, who moved into Pine Grove Manor last year with advanced dementia. "I found him shitting into the washing machine one night," Mac says with a shrug.

I get the impression that these guys come and go as they please here, treating Mac's place like more of a clubhouse than a home. It's a big house for one person. The basement is a holdover, frozen in time for as long as any of us have been alive. There's wood panelling, orange shag, oversize brown sofa segments, and worn chairs made of teak and covered in oatmeal fabric. There's a rotary phone on an end table. Mac's TV, the only modern thing in the room, is an anachronism. The whole place smells stale—stale beer, stale cigarettes, stale ambition.

These guys come here a couple times each week to drink and watch hockey. I've barely cracked my first can open when Mac disappears into a room behind the basement stairs and returns with a blowtorch, two scorched knives, and a funnel. I recognize these as the tools of obsessively efficient dope-smoking.

Sure enough, Shitty fishes a loonie from his wallet, a wad of hash stuck to the Queen's face. Is this still how it's done? I'll smoke a joint sometimes, but hash stuck to coins? Hot knives? I haven't seen, much less done, this stuff since high school. I had always assumed it was only something you did until you were old enough to know better.

Shitty pulls off small chunks of hash, balling each one up with his nicotine-stained fingers. I'm pretty sure his scuzzy Habs cap is the same one he wore in high school. He's furrier now, with a clear aversion to shaving and haircuts, but otherwise is mostly pale skin and sinew. He lines up the balls of hash with military precision, his eyes never leaving the TV.

"So, you're out west?" he asks. *Out west* is the very specific term people on the East Coast apply to everything between Toronto and Japan.

"Yeah. Calgary."

"Never been." Shitty rolls off another ball of hash and places it at the end of the line. There's a better-than-average chance he's never been farther than Halifax. "Tail's good there, I imagine." This might be a question, or it might be a general statement; an opinion of Calgary developed from afar.

"Hey, does Calgary have hookers?" Paulie asks.

"Sure, I guess," I say. "I don't use them, but they're there."

"Man, I wish we had hookers."

This cracks Mac up. "That's about the only way you'd get fucked," he says to Paulie.

"I get fucked plenty, fuckhead," Paulie snipes back. "It'd just be nice if it was easier, you know? A nice-looking piece and all it takes is twenty bucks without no hassle."

"Probably be good if she weren't your cousin, too. That'd be a nice change for you," Shitty chides.

I explain to Paulie that Calgary hookers aren't like movie hookers. They aren't Julia Roberts in thigh-high vinyl boots, at least not the ones I've seen. "Twenty bucks'll only get you a hand job in an alley."

Paulie scrunches up his face with disappointment. "Right in the alley? What if it's January?"

"Right in the alley. Even in January."

"Man, that'll shrink your sac."

"Sounds like a good date to me," says Mac.

There's more laughter all around, in the middle of which Shitty fires up the torch, dials it down to a steady blue flame, and props it between his feet on the floor. He holds the knives to the torch with his right hand and picks up the funnel with his left. The knives start glowing orange and his eyes stay glued to the TV. I consider how fast the shag carpet and wood panelling would go up if he tipped the torch or dropped a blade. As soon as the referee blows his whistle to stop the play, Shitty pops the narrow end of the funnel into his lips, takes a knife in each hand, touches one to a hash ball, which sticks, then crushes it between the blades. A puff of smoke instantly rises and disappears into the wide mouth of the funnel, nothing wasted. Like I said, efficient dope-smoking.

Shitty passes the funnel, and one by one he turns hash into puffs of smoke for everyone in the room. It's Dave that finally hands the funnel to me. I hesitate to take it from him.

"What? City boys don't smoke?" His eyes are still the darkest I've ever seen, almost black. He's added about thirty pounds of muscle since I last saw him, and keeps a well-manicured goatee, though his hair has receded, leaving a lot of forehead. His T-shirt is tight on his biceps and he's wearing too much cologne. But he's still Dave, and if there's such a thing as peer pressure for adults, I'm feeling it. As a kid, Dave was the instigator for my first cigarette, my first drink, my first fight, and more. Now here I am, a grown man, and Davey Arsehole is double-dog daring me with a simple look. And it works because some things never change.

First, I launch into an emphatic coughing fit, and then, quicker than I'd have expected, my eyes get dry and heavy, my brain sluggish. I stare into the TV, hoping it'll mask how stoned I am, but I can't follow the game at all. I know the rules of hockey and I've watched thousands of games, but right now it's moving too fast. I can't make sense of what's happening on the screen. When the Leafs score, Paulie and Shitty stand and yell, which startles me, then they start high-fiving around the room and, when it's my turn, I miss Shitty's hand entirely. I feel like a fraud, ashamed that I can't keep up.

Is someone talking to me? Someone is talking to me. It's Paulie. Paulie is talking to me. Focus on his voice. Act casual.

"Sorry? Pardon? What?" Smooth.

"Flames games? Do you go to them? In Calgary?" Paulie punctuates his sentence with pauses, turning one question into three. It seems like a deliberate attempt to mess with me.

"Yes. Well, no. Sometimes." Ugh. Does he know I'm high? Isn't he high? I feel like a monkey in a cage.

Dave jumps in, stretching the concentration I can give this conversation to the absolute limit. "Don't you have to go? Isn't that your job or whatever?"

Right. I suppose it is my job. Did I tell Paulie that? Did he tell everybody else? Wait, what's the question? Think, think, think. Go back a step. Hockey. The Flames. I don't cover the Flames, though. Shit, that's his question. Answer him, dummy.

"No!" I say with more enthusiasm than is warranted. "Not my beat."

To my right, Mac lights a cigarette. He has a spider tattoo that seems to be crawling out of his unkempt neck beard.

What does it say about someone who gets a spider tattooed on their neck? They served time in prison? They don't care about impressing potential future mothers-in-law? They eat kittens for breakfast?

"You must get free tickets or something, though," says Paulie. Are we still talking about this? I would really like to stare at Mac's tattoo for a bit. It's a terrible piece of work, faded in spots, lines too thick for any significant detail. But Mac's neck, like the rest of him, is enormous, so the tattoo artist had a lot of canvas to work with. Maybe he'll let me touch it.

I look at Paulie though droopy eyelids and a haze of smoke and brain sludge. "Sure. Sometimes." And then to Mac, "Did that hurt?"

"Did what hurt?"

"Your neck."

"Did my neck hurt?"

"The thing. On your neck. The spider." I'm pointing like an idiot, my finger an inch away from his head. I want to poke the tattoo.

"Oh. No, not really."

"Why did you do that?"

"Dunno. Seemed like a good enough idea at the time. I mostly forget it's there."

When Mac inhales from his cigarette, his neck muscles tense and the spider twitches. The illusion freaks me out and I have to turn away.

Paulie is watching me. "You okay, man?"

"Yes." No. The world around me is a loud, fuzzy mess.

"You look a little pale."

"Lightweight," Dave mutters, smirking. Asshole.

Everyone is looking at me. Everyone is smirking. Assholes.

"Right baked, wha?" says Shitty, slapping my knee.

I have been found out for the non-hash-smoking poseur I am. "Were we talking about the Flames?"

They laugh and it helps. It all feels okay. We watch hockey for a while and it doesn't matter that I can't remember the beginning of each play by the time the end comes along. People talk, but I stop following the threads. I relax and try to enjoy my high.

When the game ends, we end up standing around the kitchen drinking more beer. Kitchen drinking is another one of those East Coast idiosyncrasies I'd forgotten. Mac's kitchen, like his basement, is a 1970s relic, with sea-foam-green cupboards and linoleum yellowed by time and spilled Kraft Dinner.

The guys tell stories, and my head clears enough that I can keep up. I learn what they've been up to. Besides the house, Mac also inherited his uncle's garage, where he specializes in salvaging Mustangs and Trans-Ams and other cars popular with young men in the eighties. Shitty is the janitor at West County Consolidated, the local elementary and junior high school, and lives with Danielle Morrison. Dave and Paulie are between jobs, Paulie because he is, by his own admission, "too fuckin' lazy to bother," Dave for reasons no one even hints at.

And I learn what other people I used to know ended up doing with their lives. Many stayed put, or left for school, then came right back. Jon Green works at his dad's car dealership. Chris MacKinnon is on town council, his older brother Todd is a constable with the local RCMP, and his younger brother Trevor sells hash to Shitty. Tara MacDonnell and Kent MacDonnell (no relation) got married and bought the local pizza place. Others really left. Justin "No Duh" McNeil is a lawyer in Halifax and Denny Murphy went overseas. Jason "Boner" Bonner plays in a band popular enough that I might have heard of them, but not so popular that anyone in the kitchen can remember what they're called. Henry Hillier became a professional wrestler and, last anyone heard, was performing in Florida under the name Hillbilly Hank. A few guys went to Alberta for oil-patch jobs and turn up for visits every couple of years with scads of cash. Some got married, some had kids, at least two died (brain aneurism and ATV accident), and a few, like me, just disappeared.

Hearing all this is like my drive through downtown Pennington: simultaneously familiar and not. So-and-so is working here now. Such-and-such got a new truck. Lives were lived in my absence. This world kept spinning, even without me in it.

Have these guys ever stood in this kitchen and talked about me? Seems unlikely. I want to jump in, take part, but there's nothing I can contribute. I've been gone too long. I stay quiet until I hear the name Stephanie, which provides me with an opening.

"Stephanie Smith? I saw her today." I have their attention. I am now a living, breathing part of the conversation, and all eyes are on me. Don't screw it up. "She's still kind of a bitch, eh?" I have the world's biggest, dumbest grin on my face.

No one else smiles. In fact, they seem to be gawking at me.

That's when Dave punches me in the head.

CHAPTER THREE

There's a deep purple bruise in my hairline near my right temple. It wasn't much of a fight. Dave hit me, and I, being very far from sober and not accustomed to getting punched, quickly dropped to my hands and knees in pain and confusion. When I got up, Mac had his yeti paw on Dave's chest to keep him back.

On the way back to my motel, Paulie explained that Dave and Stephanie got married, but are currently separated and it's not something Dave talks about. That said, she's still his wife and he doesn't take kindly to her being called names. Fair enough, though a warning would have been nice.

As fate has it, Dave was also the last person who punched me. High school popularity is a bit like the stock market—some stocks go up, while others crap out. Dave was a blue-chipper. I was more like the account you dump fifty bucks into for your newborn's college fund—not worthless, but entirely safe and unsexy and forgettable. I was Dave's sidekick. It didn't bug me that other people saw me that way, but when Dave acted like I was lucky he even bothered with me, it stung. It was as though I was a social obligation—someone he hung out with because he had to. I never called him on it. There are worse things than being on the fringe of popularity, like not being on the fringe of popularity.

One night in the middle of Grade 11, Dave put together a sort of double date for us with Stephanie and Gail McGuigan. We ended up drinking cheap vodka in the dugout at the baseball field on the north side of town. It was almost spring, but the nights were still cold and what snow was left on the ground was hard and icy. Dave and I passed the vodka back and forth with our mitts on, drinking straight from the bottle, trying our best not to blanch at the taste in front of the girls.

I've always been uncomfortable around women, doubly so back then, when sex was still a mystery, but I think we were having fun. We were teenage boys trying to impress teenage girls, doing the best we could to show off. Years later, after many mistakes and occasional successes, I learned there are two kinds of showing off: confident and obnoxious. Dave was at ease with girls. More importantly, he was at ease with himself. I wore life like a hand-me-down suit, struggling to fit inside my own crippling self-awareness. Sitting there with Stephanie and Gail, Dave was calm and easy-going. I was loud and desperate to impress everyone around me. The girls saw Dave and they saw me and they saw that we were different in a way that meant if we paired off in couples, the girl who ended up with me would be considered the runner-up. I didn't care. I just wanted someone to make out with.

Dave found a long stick and stood at home plate, batting rocks and clumps of ice into the outfield. I kicked a snowbank to gather up more baseball-sized chunks and pitched them to him, soft at first, which he smacked hard, then with as much force as my shoulder could manage, which he hit even harder. In the dugout, the girls tittered and cheered with each hit.

"Okay, throw to me," I said, hoping to redeem myself. Dave shrugged, dropped the stick, and headed to the mound. I took my place at the plate and swiped at the air a few times, feigning a warm-up, wiggled my ass, and leaned into an exaggerated batter's stance.

Dave tilted back and came with a hard inside pitch that grazed the arm of my coat. I flinched, then whistled to play it off. "Okay, now give me something I can actually hit," I said, and stepped back in, this time staying more upright. The next pitch came inside again, even harder, and I ducked out of the way before it hit me.

"Asshole," I shouted, but in a playful way. My plan was to make contact and trot the bases no matter how far it went. I just didn't want to whiff with the girls watching.

Another chunk of ice came toward me, this time low, hitting the ground just in front of my feet.

"You couldn't hit the ocean from the beach." I taunted him for missing the plate, but in the moonlight, I saw a look on his face that suggested his pitches were going exactly where he wanted them to.

He picked up another piece and stood tossing it up and catching it, waiting for me to step back in the box, which I did cautiously.

"One more inside and you walk me," I said, challenging him to throw a strike. I figured he was setting me up to miss when he finally sent one down the middle. I was ready. The girls went quiet. The entire world went quiet. This was my pitch.

Dave cocked, lifting his leg like a big-league pitcher, and took a long stride toward me as he threw. My ear exploded in pain. The feeling was so intense I couldn't move or hear or see. I was sure my ear was gone, the right side of my head numb around the hot crater where it used to be. I don't remember falling down, but I could feel the frigid ground through my jeans. I don't know how long I sat there, in agony and shock.

"Are you okay?" one of the girls asked, her voice barely audible over the shrill ringing in my head.

I couldn't bring myself to touch my ear. "Is it bleeding?" I asked.

Dave laughed. "No. Get up," he said. "Let's go drink beers in Mac's garage."

I sat, dizzy and nauseated. Tears welled in my eyes, and as they started to spill down my face, Dave muttered, "Jesus Christ, fucking crybaby."

"Fuck off, Dave. It hurts," I yelled.

"So, it hurts. Don't be such a pussy."

I'd seen this from him before, directed toward unlucky losers and geeks at school. Most of the time Dave was just Dave, unfuckwithable. But he could also be mean. When he decided to break a person, they were helpless to stop him. There was real cruelty inside him.

Dave and the girls left without me. I walked home by myself, my ear hot and aching, my wet face stinging in the bitter cold.

The next morning, we had early hockey practice. My ear was still red and sore to the touch, but Dave said nothing. He didn't even acknowledge me, just put on his gear, joked around with some of the other guys, and went on like nothing had happened. The longer practice went and the more nothing was said, the more I seethed.

In any break-up there's history and hurt feelings and, often, a strong desire to see bad things happen to the other person.

We were running dump-and-chase drills, and Dave got to the puck ahead of me. He was in the corner, his back turned, and, without thinking about it, I took a hard run at him. He was fine, but it was a dangerous thing to do and, from anyone else's perspective, completely unprovoked. The coaches were livid that I'd tried to injure their star player. I spent the rest of practice bag-skating. Afterward, in the dressing room, they reamed me out again before leaving my fate to the rest of the team.

"What the fuck was that?" Dave yelled after the adults were gone.

"Don't be such a pussy," I barked back, my voice shaking with rage and fear.

Dave shoved me, I shoved him, and then his fist connected with my cheekbone. Puberty is fickle and inegalitarian. I got zits and mood swings. Dave, meanwhile, had turned into a hairy beast with the kind of grown-man strength that made him impossible to knock off a puck. He had a good fifteen pounds on me. I managed to hit him exactly one time before he forced me to the ground, sat on my chest, and slapped the shit out of me. My teammates saw it as a beating I deserved and let it happen.

It was my father who pulled Dave off. I should have been grateful, but I was too humiliated, both because he saw me getting beaten up and because I clearly needed him to bail me out. The team finished changing back into street clothes and quietly left, Dave included. My father stayed in the room until it was just the two of us. He sat quietly, grey wool toque in hand. That air of disappointment only parents emit hung between us. It was probably the most fatherly moment of his life, sharing that disappointment. Considering he'd made a career of beating people up and I'd just gotten my ass kicked, I thought maybe he'd give me some advice, a couple tips that would help me in future fights. He didn't. He got up and left without a word, leaving me wounded and angry and alone in a room that smelled like sweaty teenage boys.

I quit after that morning and haven't played hockey since. Whenever I hear a retiring athlete talk about leaving the game on his own terms, I'll think, "Yeah, that's what I did. I totally left hockey on my own terms." It's a pretty stupid thing to think.

•

The fight that ended my father's career was legendary. It wasn't on any *Don Cherry's Rock'em Sock'em* videos and they never showed highlights of it on *Hockey Night in Canada*, but people liked to talk about it. Around Pennington, that fight was regarded as no less than the greatest fight in the history of hockey. Shitty used to tell us he'd seen it—that his cousin in Newfoundland had it on VHS—but after a while, when he kept failing to produce a copy, it was clear he was lying. The fight became mythical—to hear people talk about it, you'd swear Terry Punchout slew a dragon, conquered a continent, and died the noblest of deaths. The very thing that destroyed his career was also his crowning achievement. Even J.J. Johnstone, constantly banging his drum about how bad my father was for the sport in the pages of the *Record*, couldn't diminish the glory of Dad's final battle in local hearts and minds.

Of course, that's because nobody had actually seen the fight. The game wasn't televised in Canada, and the country's first specialty sports channel was still two years away from existing. I wasn't until the internet came along that video of the fight finally surfaced and everyone, including me, got to see it.

It was soon after I got to Calgary that a co-worker sent me an email with the subject "HOLY SHIT!!!" Inside there was a link to a website that specialized in collecting hockey fight videos.

The video, likely digitized from a tape that had been sitting in someone's basement for years, was grainy and choppy. It took me a few seconds to work out what it was I was even looking at. The fight didn't start out like much of anything. There was a scrum near the benches, a few players shoving and jawing at each other, and then I see my father, young again, in the thick of it.

Lars Nilsen, one of the early Swedish imports to the league, barks something at my father, the two of them nose to nose. Lars smiles and turns to skate away. My father throws down his stick and gloves, spins the Swede around by his shoulder, and swings. It's fast, and the first few punches are wild. Then, all at once, blood is everywhere. I've seen hundreds of hockey fights, but this was different —the violence more visceral. My father is bludgeoning Lars Nilsen. Nilsen never fights back, doesn't even protect himself. The blood covering his face spatters other players every time my father pulls his hand back for another shot. The referees, busy breaking up other, lesser fights, let it go longer than it should. Finally, someone on my father's own team catches his arm and pulls him away. Nilsen crumples to the ice and the video ends, freezing on my father looking at the blood dripping from his hand.

I'm reminded of the casual curiosity on his face in that video now while watching him open a folding chair with just a quick jerk. If you aren't watching closely, you wouldn't know my father's right hand barely works. He's spent over twenty years developing coping mechanisms, using just his left hand when he can, burying the scarred right hand in pockets. He can still manage a pincer grip with his thumb and forefinger, but the other digits are useless. He's built cheats into everything he does—opening doors, eating food, driving his Zamboni.

"Are you sure you want to do this here?" I ask. He's cleaned the place up in preparation, but I'm worried he still might be uneasy having me here.

"Of course. Why not? What's wrong with it? You said you needed a quiet place. It's quiet."

"Yeah, it's perfect. I just want to make sure you're comfortable."

"I'm comfortable."

"Okay."

We both look around the room at nothing in particular.

"So, should we get started?"

"Sure," he says, "or did you want to get some fries or chips downstairs first? Or a pop?"

"If you need something, sure, but I'm fine."

"Oh. Well, if you're fine, I'm fine."

"Are you sure?"

"Of course I'm sure."

If I were ranking every conversation I've ever had, this would be among the worst. We're dancing around the thing we're here to do. "Then I guess we should start," I say.

He doesn't move, and I have to reach around him to pull the folding chair over so I can sit. After a beat, he perches on his recliner, though he's at the absolute edge of the seat, rigid and tense, like he's waiting for me to deliver bad news.

I set the tape recorder on the end table next to his chair.

"That thing'll hear me?"

"It'll hear you fine, but please talk as clearly as you can."

"Talk about what?"

"You tell me. Where should we begin?"

"I have no earthly clue."

He's rubbing the scar on his hand, same as yesterday. It's like a nervous tic and he seems oblivious to it. I think of the fight that gave him the scar, and I want to ask him more about it, but that would be jumping to the end of the story. I haven't figured out what exactly it is I can write about my father that's as compelling as I need it to be. So much of what comes next for me is now riding on what's past for him. I can't risk him glossing over something valuable—I can't skip ahead.

"Let's start at the beginning," I say, pressing down the button on my tape recorder. "Tell me about where you're from."

•

You already know I'm from here.

...

Well, what the hell is the point of me telling you stuff you already know?

...

My own words? Well, who the Christ else's words would I use?

...

Fine, fine. I was born just outside of town here—the south side, in 1947. Do you need that stuff, too, my birthday and such? Maybe every time I took a shit?

...

So, 1947. My folks raised Cotswolds—that's sheep—on a small farm just south of town. I must've been only four or five when Dad started getting me to hold the sheep down for shearing. He didn't need to, or at least, he managed just fine before I come along, but the truth is I think he got a kick out of it, watching me wrestle with the goddamned things. He'd holler at me and I'd wrap my arms around some mutton's neck to drag him down to the ground. "The legs, boy, get the legs," he'd holler, but I was scared of the legs. Ever been kicked by a full-size Cotswold?

...

Well, it hurts something fierce. Won't kill you, but you learn not to get kicked twice. I'd take them down by the head.

...

No, Dad never knew how to skate and didn't have time for things like hockey. He was always working around the farm, and I honestly can't say what he did with the time when he wasn't. It was Mum who got me the skates and it was Mum who showed me how to use them. Make sure you put that in this thing you're writing. She'd've liked that.

...

Well, just mention it somewhere in there. You didn't know your gran, but she was a nice lady. I got the skates for Christmas. They were old brown leather things, and goddamned if they weren't five sizes too big, so Mum stuffed newspaper into the toes and walked with me on the ice, holding my arms while I figured out my legs. I was on that pond for, Jesus, must have been seven or eight years. I hammered together a net out of old wood and would shoot at it for hours. I finally got a new pair of skates when I was about thir-

teen and I begged Dad to let me play hockey in town. Mum didn't drive, so it was him who'd need to take me in for games and practices and such. He wasn't keen on it, but he agreed. I always supposed Mum made him do it. Playing hockey came easy to me. It was those years of skating on the pond and wrestling with the sheep. I showed up and was better than the lot of 'em. I wasn't a great puck handler, so I'd cut my stick short and cradle the puck close to my body. Then I could push my way through other kids and I always had a pretty good shot. That first year, I scored whenever I wanted to, so the next winter, they made me play with the older kids, thinking it'd be more fair. Well, I was better than all of them, too.

...

Mr. Asmus was the name of the man who scouted me. I never caught his first name—Dad just said, "This is Mr. Asmus and he thinks you should play hockey in Toronto next year." He wore a sharp blue suit and smoked those cigars that are small like cigarettes. Had a big ol' smile on his face pretty much all the time. Those scouts aren't really scouts at all. They're salesmen. I scored fifty-four goddamned goals that year. Most in the league. It's not like he needed to make some kind of judgment on my talent. I was better than anyone else playing juniors in Nova Scotia, so he showed up to convince my folks to let me play juniors in Ontario. That was his whole job: convincing mums to let their sons go.

...

No, Mum wasn't keen on it at all. I think Dad was mostly surprised—the idea that I'd get to Toronto for hockey, of all things. Anyways, he said it was my choice and my choice alone. There was something about the way he said it, like he didn't think I had the stomach for it. And he wasn't all wrong—I was scared shitless. It wasn't something I'd admit or something any of us boys would talk about, but I suspect we all missed our mums. I'd be damned I was gonna let him make a chickenshit out of me, though. So I told Mr. Asmus I'd love to be a Marlie and that was that. I near pissed myself when I got off the train, I was so scared. It was all so big and moved so fast. They put me in a boarding house with seven other fellas from the team, most from small towns like me, some from places I'd never heard of in Saskatchewan or New Brunswick. We got on okay, but it was still lonely at the start. Mostly we'd play cards. Can you imagine the likes of that? Bunch of kids in the big city for the first time and all we did was sit around playing euchre for nickels.

...

The hockey part didn't start so good for me. I was so used to being the best guy on the ice, but I wasn't even close with those fellas. It's a whole league of guys who were the best players from wherever they was from. It was clear pretty quick there wasn't anything special about me. I was smaller and slower and couldn't buy myself a goal. It was about a month into the season, and it didn't look like I was gonna stick. They were ready to ship me home and I was just about ready to go.

...

Our captain was Billy McGee. He was a big kid from Manitoba and he had the smoothest hands in the O— that's what we called the OHA. I guess they call it the CHL now, but we just called it the O. Anyways, McGee could really fly. He went on to get drafted by the Flyers, then he broke his leg and it never healed right. Not sure where he ended up after that. I suppose back in Bumfuck, Manitoba. Anyways, like I said, he was our captain, and the best guy we had, and one game he took a stick to the mouth. Cut him up real bad, cost him some teeth. Guy who sticked him was some French arsehole, Jacques or Pierre or whatever.

...

I don't care, he was a sleazy fuckin' frog.

...

You want me to tell the story or not? So, Billy was a good guy. I liked him and I didn't like that French bastard laughing about making him bleed. I had nothing to lose letting him know that, neither. So a couple shifts later I grabbed Pierre and beat the holy hell out of him. That was my first-ever hockey fight. My first anything fight, really. Next period they sent a guy after me to square things up and sure enough I got the best of him, too. Word got around and the next game somebody else decided to try me on for size. After that, it became a bit of a regular thing.

...

Well, for a long time I had surprise on my side. I wasn't the biggest fella, so I don't think they thought I had a lot to offer in a fight. But the secret to fighting ain't being big or strong. It's balance. I've got a nice, low centre of gravity and a real strong core. All those years doing chores and wrestling sheep gave me good control over myself. Guys today think they're in good shape because they got the six-pack stomach, well, I never had no six-pack stomach. But I don't think any of those six-packs could knock me over even now. Balance, especially on skates. You have that, no man on earth can push you around.

...

I was real popular once I started dropping my gloves. Coaches took a liking to me, and so did the other players. I carved out my place on the team, and I guess that made everything easier. Made me miss home less, helped me relax and enjoy myself a bit. At the time I expected playing in the O would be all the hockey I'd get, and I liked that it kept me off the farm most of the year. When I went home after that first year, Dad decided to have a big chat about what I was gonna do with my life. I told him I was going to go back to Toronto and play hockey for as long as they'd have me, and when they wouldn't, well, I'd sort it out then. Wasn't really the answer he was looking for. He wasn't much fun to be around after that, let me tell you. But that's also the summer I met Vivian, so I spent more time with her, anyway. Did you know your mum was a full inch taller than me? I bought thick-soled shoes after our first date.

...

Well, I can't hardly pretend she wasn't there.

...

You want me to tell you what happened and I'm telling you what happened. You can't also tell me how to tell it.

...

That summer I'd get up early to get all the choring done and rush out to spend the rest of my day with Viv. We'd go swimming or just for a drive. I didn't really have many friends, but we'd get around with hers sometimes. It didn't matter, we'd just have fun, and then in the fall I got back on the train to Toronto for another season with the Marlies.

•

Pennington has a few churches, putting everyone into neat Christian boxes. Really, though, it's a town of lapsed Catholics, Presbyterians, Anglicans, and so on, as none of them pull any kind of crowd.

My mother was raised Catholic and, I think, genuinely believed all the things she'd been told about God and Jesus and so on. My father was born Protestant, but for all intents and purposes, he was an atheist from early on. He did go to church on Sundays with his parents, but only until he was old enough to refuse, and they didn't see much point in fighting him on it. When my parents got married, it was important to my mother to have the wedding inside the church, or more specifically, St. Patrick's Church on Highland Drive. My father consented, but Father Tim, the priest at St. Patrick's, wasn't keen on people from his congregation marrying non-Catholics. For those marriages, he mandated a series of counselling sessions between himself and the otherwise happy couple.

During one of these sessions, my father made his lack of faith known. To Father Tim, non-Catholics were misguided, non-Christians were to be pitied, and atheists—what he called "the aggressively Godless"—were beneath contempt. He tried to refuse my parents a Catholic ceremony, but my mother begged and, technically, as a baptized Protestant, my father was a qualified Christian. The priest eventually acquiesced. On the day of the wedding, he told my mother that, personally, he disapproved, and more importantly, he felt God disapproved. He told her the marriage would fail and that he couldn't guarantee the salvation of any children produced by such a union. My mother got the wedding at St. Patrick's she'd always dreamed of, but she only entered a Catholic church three more times in her life—once for each of her parents' funerals and, finally, for her own, though I don't know if that last one counts.

Raised without religion, I had to work out my own worldview. What I came up with was this: everything in life is pass or fail. I don't do percentages. Things either are or they aren't. My father was a hockey player and then he wasn't. Dave and I were friends and then we weren't. My mother was healthy and then she wasn't.

We found out just before Christmas. She was tired and had lost a few pounds. She thought she had a bug she just couldn't shake and joked about her six-month flu. Eventually she went to see Dr. Kelly. He wanted tests. He wanted to take blood, to X-ray and scan things, and to cut out a small piece of her. Something was wrong.

Everything was wrong.

Her chances wouldn't have been all that great even if they had caught it early, but she had waited so long that when they did start a treatment, odds of survival were never really discussed. I was seventeen when I learned that aggressive chemotherapy isn't pretty. My mother went from not feeling well to being unable to do much more than lie in bed, which she complained hurt her back, though she couldn't muster the strength to get up most days. Her skin, always pale, took on a translucence that didn't seem real. At first, they let her come home between treatments, but near the end she was in the hospital full-time. She slept a lot, and I'd sit and watch her breathing as it became increasingly shallow. In March, my acceptance letter from St. Mary's arrived in the mail.

"I suppose I'll have to get better before you go," she said. "I don't want you worrying about me instead of studying."

I'd waited years for that letter, for the possibility of heading out into a greater world full of all the things Pennington didn't have. I wanted excitement and sophistication and interesting people, and while I wasn't sure what any of that meant in practical terms—it's not like I thought I'd be eating sushi with famous artists and going to the opera every night—I knew I had to get as far away as I could. I'd spent my entire life living in a place that never felt right.

My mother hadn't explicitly told me I had to go to university. She'd spent years asking me what I wanted to be when I grew up and was delighted by my answers, even during the brief period when I was seven and thought Pizza

Guy sounded pretty cool. Once I hit high school, she'd ask about schools and classes and majors I might be interested in. Until she got sick, not going to school wasn't an option. But I knew she wouldn't get better. My mother was sick and that meant I was stuck in Pennington because what else could I do? I wanted to blame the cancer instead of her, but as the disease ate away at her—at who she used to be—it got hard to tell the two apart and hard not to blame her for taking away all the things she'd taught me to want in the first place.

But I never had to make a choice. By April, the doctors gave up trying to fix her, because treating the thing that was killing her was only killing her faster. They told us—me and Mom and all the neighbours and distant aunts and uncles and cousins who were suddenly around me all the time— she would die, giving her anywhere from two to six months. Maybe longer, if she was lucky.

"These things can be hard to predict," the doctor told me. She died two weeks later, an unfairness I've held against all doctors everywhere ever since.

My mother was alive and then she wasn't.

•

It's six o'clock when I leave the rink with about a half-hour's worth of tape of my father. I worried I'd have trouble getting him to talk—he's not exactly a chatty guy—but as soon as I clicked the tape recorder on, he just went off with almost no prompting. It was a huge relief, and I'm feeling good when I go to meet Paulie and the guys.

Pat's Pub is a local institution. It maintains a delicate balance between respectable family restaurant during the day and the hub of Pennington's singles scene at night. As the town's only real bar, it services a wide demographic of men and women aged anywhere from nineteen to forty-five. By leaving town when I did, I never had the chance to properly take part in Pennington's nightlife, missing out on the chance to have sex with the kind of older women who spend their time at Pat's. Every choice has a consequence.

I had always imagined Pat's at night was a heady mix of disco lights and sexual possibility. In reality, transitioning "Pat's Pub for Family-Friendly Grub" to "Pat's Pub for Decisions You'll Regret Tomorrow" is a trick of dimming the lights and clearing out a half-dozen tables to create a functional dance floor. I'm sipping a rum and Coke in a corner booth, watching a waitress replace the salt and pepper shakers with ashtrays. A pair of colourful lights start moving overhead. The music isn't on yet and I can hear the gears inside grinding as beams of blue and yellow sashay back and forth across the tile floor.

There was a pub in Calgary that a few of us from work would head to on Friday nights, but it's been a while since I've been in a nightclub, even a makeshift one like Pat's. When I was younger, and dancing and drinking were prerequisites to getting laid, I'd go to clubs begrudgingly. The screaming to be heard over the music, watered-down booze, and self-consciousness over my demonstrable lack of rhythm never made it much fun. But it was the easiest way to meet girls.

My dating life is unspectacular, which, I like to point out, is different from non-existent. Before I left Calgary, Jana and I had been together for about six months. We sort of fell into the relationship by accident and neither of us worked up the momentum to break free of it. When I met her, she liked clubs and bars and going out and having fun. After a month with me, it was Saturday nights at the video store, where we'd spend over an hour trying to agree on a film. Her apartment was nicer than mine, so we spent our time there. When I told her I was leaving Calgary, she seemed relieved. It's not the response you'd expect after spending six months sleeping together. On the drive to Pennington, I had a lot of time to think about why it didn't work out, and why we couldn't recognize it soon enough to cut each other loose, no harm, no foul. Best I can figure, we just didn't have that spark or chemistry or whatever horseshit people who believe in a sappy kind of love talk about. Why isn't it enough that we got along okay, had similar enough interests, and a decent amount of pretty okay sex? If you have all of those things, and they make you happy enough, what's the difference between that and real, true, honest-to-goodness love?

Friday night is pretty shaking in Pennington. Paulie and Shitty arrive at Pat's just as the music starts—a menagerie of dated and predictable club hits—and I'm a few drinks deep. Shitty complains about his janitor job. He's developed a healthy contempt for the disgusting nature of children. "Why do those greasy little shits stick gum to everything?" And then Dave arrives with Mac. I tense up as they pile into the booth, but no one says anything about last night, not even a hint that less than twenty-four hours ago this guy's fist was travelling toward my skull with speed and conviction. Dave doesn't look at me at all, and I'm fine with that. We're in silent agreement to pretend it didn't happen.

So we drink. Again. We drink while talking about everything and nothing in particular. Mac and Dave break off to chase girls, Paulie and Shitty stay in the booth talking about girls they'd like to chase.

"Do you think Stacey will be out tonight?" Paulie asks.

"Jesus Christ, guy. You need to let that go," replies Shitty.

"What?" says Paulie, incredulous.

Shitty shakes his head and turns to me. "So get this. We're round Mac's at New Year's and Paulie manages to pick up Stacey Bailey." He makes sure I remember who Stacey is, and I nod. "Anyway, he claims he fucked her, but who's to say, right?"

"I did!" Paulie protests.

"Yeah, sure, and ever since he's always asking about her like a fucking puppy dog looking for a treat."

"Maybe he likes her," I say, defending Paulie. "But if that was New Year's, I think you can move on. She ain't interested."

Shitty laughs. "It wasn't last New Year's. We're coming up on three years since our little boy here popped his cherry. I tell you, she must have fucked him, because it's the only explanation. No one else has and the poor prick is scared no one else will."

"You've been fucking the same girl for ten years," says Paulie. "So what do you know about it, fuckhead."

"Actually, it's only been eight. Danielle wouldn't let me the first two. She's a lady."

Shitty and Danielle Morrison started dating near the end of high school, shortly before I left town. Their current relationship status is something he calls "pre-engaged." As he's explaining exactly what that is, someone slams into the booth, shoving me over. I turn to yell "Fuck off!" at the culprit and get as far as "Fuck" before I see that it's Jennifer Clark.

Jennifer could arguably be called the love of my life, not because our high school romance was Shakespearean or anything, but because there just aren't any other real contenders. The last decade has been kind to her. She's put on some weight, but it suits her. She was never much for makeup, which still seems to be true, and her brown hair is as long and thick as ever. She perfected the girl-next-door look a long time ago. Simply put, she's lovely.

"Didn't you used to be Adam Macallister," she says with a cool smile. "I knew that guy once upon a time."

"Jennifer. Hi. Wow. Hi."

"Hi."

"Hey!" Paulie shouts from the other side of the booth. "Didn't you guys used to screw?" He and Shitty fall over each other in a fit of giggles.

Jennifer doesn't miss a beat. "That's not entirely true," she says, and I'm sure the look on my face is one of abject horror.

•

Jennifer and I dated early in our Grade 12 year. She was fantastic, self-confident, fiercely independent and, in most ways, completely out of my league. But she never liked hockey players and I'd quit being one the year before, so I held a certain appeal. Our relationship progressed, as these things do. Despite my exposure to junior high sex-ed classes, locker room talk, and soft-core pornography, the specifics of sex still didn't quite fit together for me. Like, I knew what it was in a strictly mechanical sense, but the bigger questions of "How?" eluded me. I assume it's like this for everyone, but maybe I was a bit thick.

We agreed to do it through an awkward discussion with a lot of avoiding what "it" was and then a lot of making certain each other understood the "it" we weren't talking about. Jennifer's little brother, Scott, had a hockey tournament in Halifax, and their parents took him, leaving Jennifer alone for a weekend. I came over around seven. We watched *True Romance* on VHS and even though we'd seen it a thousand times, we watched it through to the end. I was terrified. We started kissing, which would normally escalate fairly quickly to heavy petting, but that night each step took forever. We made out for an hour until Jennifer, possibly realizing I wouldn't make the move, took control. She stood us up and pulled off her sweater. I did the same with my T-shirt. She undid her jeans and I undid mine. I felt silly standing in my boxer shorts, fully erect and scared to death I'd screw up putting on the condom. Jennifer undid her bra and pulled her pink panties over her hips and let them fall, stepping out gracefully. I froze and she smiled and I blushed. She stepped forward and kissed me while hooking her thumbs into my boxers. She started to sink to her knees, pulling the shorts down as she went. I felt her breath on my neck, down my chest and my stomach and...

The subject of premature ejaculation isn't covered in locker rooms or soft-core porn. It was, however, mentioned in sex ed as a thing that happens, not uncommonly. But I was sure it wouldn't happen to me. Like most guys, I had a good idea it was something to be ashamed of. Ashamed. I didn't know the meaning of the word until I accidentally came in Jennifer Clark's eye. The moment seared itself into my brain and, to this day, thinking about it brings on crushing embarrassment. What followed, however, has a more dreamlike quality. Jennifer, surprised, screamed. I said nothing, not even "I'm sorry." I grabbed my clothes and ran.

I avoided Jennifer for about a week, and when she finally tracked me down, I dumped her. It was just easier than discussing what had happened or, worse, risking it happening again. A couple months later she started dating Phil Mumford, who also didn't play hockey, but did play piano and guitar. In grade school that made him a loser, but in high school he learned some Red Hot Chili Peppers songs, and that guitar got him any girl he wanted. In March, word got out that Jennifer was pregnant. It was scandalous news in a town like Pennington, where everybody knows everybody else. While I certainly didn't want to be anyone's father at that age, I was jealous that Phil Mumford could manage what I couldn't, even if he did screw up putting on the condom. Jennifer was starting to show when I left town a few months later.

I wouldn't say I've pined after her all these years, but it's not like I haven't thought about her either. I've replayed that night in her basement in my head nearly every day, starring an infinitely more couth version of myself. I've also imagined accidentally bumping into her on the streets of Vancouver or Toronto or Montreal, where I suggest grabbing a drink someplace nice and impress her with my cosmopolitan ways. Whether by time travel or coincidence, all I wanted was a second chance—the opportunity to prove I've become something more than the sexually immature teenager she once knew. I have thought about this, but I never believed the moment would really come, and here it is, Jennifer rubbing elbows with me in a small, crowded bar and the best I can manage is "hi wow hi." Honestly, it's a wonder I've ever managed to get a girl to sleep with me at all.

CHAPTER FOUR

I'm hungover again and embarrassed by the memories seeing Jennifer dredged up. I'm bad with embarrassing memories, especially the ones that involve girls. There's the time I farted in front of Sabrina Turner in the back of her brother's car, or when I threw up after riding the Spider at the carnival in front of Nicole Bernard and Angela Cox, or when I mixed up okra and Oka during a dinner conversation with Jana and her parents while I was trying to sound smart about food—these moments pop into my head with a regularity that borders on pathological. But thinking about that night in Jennifer's basement sends me into a cold sweat every single time. My boozy headache and profound humiliation keep me in bed longer than I should be. I was supposed to meet my father around nine, but it's shortly after noon by the time I finally get moving.

The shower in my room at the Goode Night Inn has some quirks. Finding a temperature between scalding and freezing is like trying to crack a safe, and the water gushes with enough force that I have to take a step back when it slams into my chest. It's like being pressure-washed, the dirt and stink peeling away. I could stand here forever, blasting off layers of yesterdays, but there's only about six minutes' worth of hot water.

Wiping the steam from the mirror, I catch my own eye. I look tired. I look like a guy who's been drunk for days. And I'm starting to look out of shape. I've always had a thin frame, but now I'm doughy through the middle, not fat, but definitely paunchy. My various parts are soft and bleed into each other with no real definition.

Sportswriters tend to be either skinny nerds or loud fat guys. I'm sure there are a few guys that want to grow up to be Red Fisher, but most of us had other plans and instead fail into this gig. Near the end of my English degree, I wanted to be the Canadian John Steinbeck, and I managed to get one short story published in a small literary journal nobody reads. I started writing for the St. Mary's school newspaper because of some girl, and I knew a lot about hockey and baseball and football, and it turned out I could write a pretty good sentence. I don't remember ever making the decision to be a sportswriter, but somewhere along the way I became one of those guys who makes sports out to be more important than they really are because otherwise we'd have to admit a lot of uncomfortable truths to ourselves. Writing about sports—watching them closely, analyzing them, coming up with eloquent and original ways to describe the things that happen over and over and over—is a profession that belongs almost entirely to men who could never have played anything at a high level. We are the uncoordinated and the talentless. And if you're uncoordinated and talentless, but you love sports, learning to write about them is as close you'll get to being the athlete your childhood self wanted to grow up to be. We're the kids who collected hockey cards and pored over the stats on the back. I spent forty bucks each year on updated editions of *The Complete Hockey Almanac*, a gargantuan tome featuring every piece of statistical information the NHL has ever produced. I obsessed over those books and, by the time I was twelve, had committed nearly every NHL record to memory. I know that Larry Robinson is plus-730 for his career and Ian Turnbull is the only defenceman to score five goals in a game. Glenn Hall played 502 consecutive complete games as a goalie. Most points in a game by a rookie? A tie between brothers Peter and Anton Stastny, who each managed eight in the same game on February 8, 1985. Most game misconducts in a playoff series? Five: Terry Macallister, 1974.

The truth is, we're just big fans—the biggest fans—which is strange because in every other kind of journalism, there's a certain expectation of objectivity. We fake it, but deep down we're not all that different from every other diehard homer and athlete starfucker. It's all good so long as you don't get caught asking for an autograph. The downside is that after you spend a few years covering finely tuned athletes—and their muscles and talent and fame and success and money—it starts to chip away at your self-esteem. Maybe that's why guys like J.J. Johnstone end up attacking guys like my father: simple jealousy.

Not that high self-esteem has ever been a problem for me. So far in my career, I've been lucky to get assigned to cover university volleyball games. Even after I was hired as a full-time reporter, most of my bylines are community colour pieces: "Minor Hockey Team Raises $6,000 Selling Apples" or "Junior Curlers Hope to Play for Provincial Medals." I wrote filler—stories mothers could cut out about their kids and stick up on the fridge. But I was paid money to watch people play games and write about them, which is pretty good. I'd been angling to get on the Major Junior hockey beat, covering the Calgary Hitmen and the NHL draft prospects, when the layoffs came. The internet has made even the cushiest newspaper jobs tenuous, never mind positions for low-level guys like me. I wasn't all that surprised when the axe finally came down, though I really should have had some kind of backup plan in place. Instead, I took my two weeks' severance and sat on my ass until my lack of savings became a real problem.

I was in a bar watching the Leafs play the Stars when a graphic showing Bobby Monahan's pursuit of my father's record popped up. The light bulb went off. I remember saying, "What happened to Terry Punchout?" out loud, followed by, "Fuck." I'd thought about writing about my father before, but was never sure he was interesting enough. But the moment presented me with the perfect combination of relevance—his falling record—and desperation— my failing career. I'm self-aware enough to know I've got a half-baked scheme that doesn't stand up to a lot of scrutiny, so I try not to scrutinize it. If this goes sideways, I'm unemployed in a shrinking industry with few prospects and no favours to cash in.

After a few minutes of feeling bad about the way I look, my current employment status, not having had sex with Jennifer Clark ten years ago (or last night), and a half-dozen other things, I brush my teeth and put on the same shirt I wore yesterday. On my way to the rink, I stop for coffees, hoping it'll both tame my hangover and keep the peace with my father, given how late I am.

•

When I get to the rink, my dad isn't in his apartment. I roam the building for about ten minutes before I find him in the small Zamboni room. The front of the machine is open, tilted forward, and pouring snow into a large hole in the floor straddled by the Zamboni's tires. I've never seen this before—I've never even thought about how a Zamboni actually works—so it had never occurred to me that the large, boxy front was almost entirely empty most of the time.

"How many times do you have to clean the ice to fill that thing?"

"You're late," my father says as the snow finishes emptying. He slaps a switch with his bad hand and the front of the machine lowers itself back into place with a low whir.

"Yeah, sorry. Late night. You know how it is," I say with a weak smile, recognizing that he probably doesn't know how it is. He crouches down next to the Zamboni and opens a panel on the side. "But I brought you some coffee." I hold the cup out toward him, but he doesn't look up, so I set it down on a narrow table to my left covered with tools, some tubes, and other bits and pieces of machinery, most of which are foreign to me. I've never been mechanically inclined.

"So," I say after several minutes of silence, "do you want to talk here, or should I wait for you upstairs?"

"No time. Game's at two-thirty."

"I know, me and some of the guys were gonna meet up at the bar and then come down and watch it. But you and I have some time first."

"No, we don't," he says coldly. "The peewees just went on and I'll need to clean the ice as soon as they finish, which means I've got an hour to fix the vacuum on this thing."

"The vacuum?"

"Yes, the vacuum. It sucks up the wash water. If you don't suck up the wash water, you leave dirt on the ice."

"Right. Dirt." It's clear the machine is old—it looks like the same one from when I was young, which would make it at least twenty years. How many hours has my father put into patching it up? How many times has he fixed the same vacuum? When did he get so handy with machines?

"Look, Dad, we've got to get these interviews done. I've only got so much time, you know?"

"Then you should get out of bed earlier."

"Jesus. I thought we decided you weren't going to be like this."

My father stops tinkering inside the machine and looks up at me from where he's squatting. "Be like what?"

"Like this," I say. "A letdown."

"You need to stop acting like I owe you this, boy. I don't. You want some of my time, fine. But right now I need to get the fucking vacuum working, whether that's disappointing to you or not."

"I knew this would happen. Why would I be able to count on you for something now?" I feel petulant and I don't know where it's coming from. Is this what unrepressed anger feels like? It's satisfying.

My father sighs and his eyes fall away from mine. "Adam, you can be mad as hell about what you think I did or didn't do, but it doesn't change the fact that right now I have to get this goddamn thing working." He punctuated that last bit by kicking the side of the Zamboni.

This would be a good time to walk out. I could go, meet the guys, have a drink, and watch the game. Come back tomorrow and pretend this conversation didn't happen. No real harm has been done here. Yet. I turn to go, but something in me just can't leave it alone.

"This is why she left you, isn't it? Shit like this. You were just a constant letdown, so she left you."

My father stands. The arch in his back straightens, and he seems to grow a full two inches, looking more like the man I remember.

"She didn't leave me. We just needed..." he pauses, searching for the right words "...to be apart for a bit."

"A bit! You were divorced for fifteen years when she..." Died, but I can't finish the sentence out loud.

"It was more complicated than that."

"Yeah? I bet it was pretty easy for her."

"Nothing like that comes easy."

"So, what was it? What made her go?"

"Nothing," he says, but a slight dip in his shoulders betrays him, and I know I'm onto something. His discomfort eggs me on.

"There was something, wasn't there?"

"No."

"Did you hit her?"

"I would never!" The fire in his eyes tells me he's not lying.

"So what? You cheated on her?" Again, he deflates a little. "Holy shit! You did. You fucking bastard."

"I made bad choices."

"You fucked someone else."

"I behaved inappropriately."

"Jesus, you can't even say it."

"It doesn't need to be said."

And I suppose it doesn't. He's wounded and on the ropes, and if I wanted, I could take out years of frustration and anger on him. I could yell and scream and use my mother—the memory of her—to cut him to his core. And I can tell he knows this. But, mad as I am, using my mother to break him seems unconscionably cruel. It would also be a pyrrhic victory—I could hollow out what little is left of him, but it would leave me with nothing, too. No interview, no article, no real ties to my hometown.

"Look, I'm gonna go—we can both cool off, you can get your work done, or whatever. But after the game, can we try again?" I hate that I need him more than he needs me right now. "Please."

My father slowly walks over to the workbench and picks up a tool. "Come by here an hour after the game is done," he says with his back to me.

•

The Duke Street house was a gift from the town, a property they owned for some reason or other, but was rundown and unused. They told him he could stay there rent-free until he sorted himself out. Everyone knew he was coming home broke, but no one talked about why. He left when he was sixteen and became a celebrity. Pennington was excited to have him back.

I was excited to have him back, too. We'd finally get to do all the things fathers and sons did, which, in my mind, involved a lot of playing catch and fishing and watching hockey. I imagined these were the things all sons did with their dads, even though I had no real evidence. Dave's dad wasn't around any more than mine, Paulie's was a dick, and the rest were just sort of there. But a kid's mind is like a rock tumbler: ideas go in, bounce around, and come out polished and shiny, but in the end, they're still just rocks. My idea was that, somehow, in complete defiance of history and probability and evidence, my dad would become Father of the Year on his return. It really pissed me off when he didn't.

The first month or so was good. He seemed happy to be around and talked a lot about what he was going to do. "No free rides," he'd say. "We should fix this old house up a bit. Want to help your old man do that, Skinny?" Yes, Dad. "Maybe I'll go coach the Royals. I could teach those kids a thing or two, right, Skinny?" Yes, Dad. "Hell, maybe I'll run for mayor! Think I'd make a good mayor, Skinny?" Yes, Dad.

I begged my mother to let me stay with him on weekends, and much as it probably pained her, she couldn't come up with a good reason not to. My father and I would watch hockey and play cards. He'd take me with him around town and, wherever we went, people wanted to shake his hand, welcoming him home, while I stood there beaming with pride.

But gradually my father wore down. Fewer people wanted to say hello because everyone had already said hello. It became clear that the town, accommodating as it was, had no plan for him, and my dad, for all his talk about coaching and politicking, didn't have one for himself.

He'd drink rum and Cokes all night, and while he wasn't a sloppy drunk, even at eight years old I could tell when he had a lop on, especially if we were watching hockey. The drunker he got, the more he'd yell at players and referees, using nicknames and first names because he knew most of them. More often than not, he'd fall asleep in his chair, snoring loudly, and I'd turn off the TV and go to bed. Within a year, we'd made a routine of our weekends together. TV. Rum. Snore. Bed. He wasn't much for keeping the fridge stocked, and on the nights we didn't get pizza, I was left to eat ketchup sandwiches.

His relationship with Pennington fell into the same kind of routine. Terry Punchout went from being a local legend to being a local fixture, more of a mascot than a hero. The town was nice enough about it, though, letting him keep the house even though he hadn't done anything to earn it. His idea about coaching the Royals seemed reasonable to me, and probably most everyone else. I think people assumed it was going to happen, but they never officially asked, so Dad never officially offered. In his mind, that would have been asking for a handout. He was fine with using the house, because he hadn't asked for it, which I suppose fit with his antiquated notions of respect and manliness and how people should conduct themselves. You can probably blame hockey for those ideas, too.

•

I climb the stairs to J.J.'s to meet the guys before the Royals game at two-thirty. The bar is much busier than the last time I was here. Every Royals game is a minor event in this town, but Saturday-afternoon games are like church. I have to admit, putting a bar in this rink was a stroke of genius. I have no idea who gets the money from the booze sales, but it's clear the Royals might be the linchpin of the entire Pennington economy, as the bar is already filling up and I know the seats inside the arena will be at capacity.

Because I'm early, I manage to snag a table. Shitty applauds my initiative when he arrives, happy he doesn't have to carry his pitcher of beer around the crowded bar. I've already got one on the go, but Shitty orders another three and puts them on the table. Paulie and Mac show up and each adds two more. Dave buys himself one bottled beer and avoids our table.

The bar is filled almost entirely with men. The older guys share stories about goals scored, fish caught, women bedded, and days won. People ask each other about wives and mothers and kids as though they hadn't all done this just a week ago. Like last night, I'm left at the table with Paulie, while the other guys make the rounds. Paulie humours people who stop to chat, answering questions in a way that isn't answering them at all.

"How's your mum?"

"Oh, you know Mum."

"And what are you up to, Paul?"

"Oh, just a bit of this and that."

Then they give a little laugh and move on. Meanwhile, Paulie's father is working the room as hard as anyone, answering the same questions about his wife ("Healthy as a horse") and what his son is up to these days ("Not so much working hard as he is hardly working"). Mac and Shitty come by the table often to refill their glasses and, in Shitty's case, roll his eyes in a way that isn't specific, but is perfectly clear: this show—men meeting and drinking and being social with expired braggadocio and vapid small talk—is ridiculous. It's all patter and platitudes, and while I suspect this is the way all men talk when they spend time together, that these men choose to do this every single weekend boggles my mind.

"Is it always like this?" I ask Paulie.

He takes a second to size up the room, trying to figure out what it is I'm really asking. I think he gets it. "Yeah. I guess," he says, and shrugs.

"And you guys do this every weekend?"

"What the hell else would we do?"

"I don't know, but you'd think you'd be tired of this. It's just a bunch of assholes trying to relive their glory days, isn't it?"

Paulie screws up his face in a way that implies he's never really given the ritual much serious consideration. "Yeah, I s'pose that's about right."

"And you don't get sick of that?"

"Not really. Makes them happy, we get to have a few drinks, so what are ya gonna do?"

About thirty minutes before the game starts, J.J. Johnstone himself walks into the bar named for him. J.J. was always a large man, but now he's fantastically fat. He's wearing a fur coat and a boxy fur hat, which seems like overkill for early November. The only skin you can see is his bulbous pink face, his chins stacked like folded bath towels. He moves like a planet through the crowded bar, dragging a small group of men, Paulie's dad among them, behind him like moons. J.J. moves a few feet and stops to shake hands, moves a few more feet and does it again. You'd think he was running for public office. If there were a baby, he'd kiss it, dooming the poor thing to a lifetime of nightmares involving sweaty pink furry balloon monsters. When he reaches the windows overlooking the rink, a group of people clear out, leaving seats for him and his cronies. Someone comes along and takes his coat. The whole thing feels like a bad imitation of *The Godfather*.

Mac and Shitty come back to the table and sit, looking tired from their social travels. Mac takes a long pull from his beer and immediately refills it. Shitty takes a half-full pitcher and drinks straight from it. I notice Dave has made his way to over to J.J.'s mafia circle, smiling and chatting with a stiff posture that doesn't quite suit him.

"Jesus, what's that about?" I ask.

"Oh, those guys love Dave," says Paulie. "He's as good at telling stories as any of them."

"Kid's gotta earn that walking-around money," says Shitty. Paulie snorts, but Mac gives them both a stern look and they quiet down.

"They give him money?" Shit, maybe they really are like the mafia.

Paulie tilts his head back and forth. "Not a lot. J.J. and Dad and those guys are sort of like boosters. They take care of the players."

Shitty laughs, "Yeah, boosters. They've been boosting Arsehole's wallet since he was seventeen."

"It's none of our business," says Mac.

Shitty puts his hands up and opens his mouth mockingly, but doesn't actually say anything.

"I gotta piss," says Mac, putting his beer down and moving away.

Mac was the only other one of us who played for the Royals. He was too big not to put on the team and was a pretty good defenceman. Growing up, Mac was always Dave's protection. Whenever someone had the nerve to take a poke, Mac would be there instantly, imposing his will, as well as his giant right fist. It wasn't any different off the ice. One weekend there was a party at Beth Gillis's house and three guys from New Glasgow showed up looking for Davey Arsehole for reasons involving one of their girlfriends. They found Mac first. He broke a guy's nose and escorted him out by his hair, the two buddies following behind quietly after deciding whoever's honour they were defending wasn't worth it. Dave never even saw them before Mac had them on their way home.

"Did Dave ever try to leave town to play?" I ask. "Major Junior or university hockey?" Dave was talented and, much as I might not like the guy, watching him suck up to J.J. for a handout bothers me. Shouldn't he have done more? Dave was a dick, sure, but he was also a good hockey player.

"Yeah. He went to some place in Quebec," says Shitty. "Got cut after a couple weeks."

"He really wasn't good enough?"

"I don't know, he probably was. But he don't want to be just another player in some fuckhole town when he could be the best player in this fuckhole town," Shitty says, evoking a strong sense of Pennington pride.

"He went to St. Thomas, too," Paulie adds. "When he was too old for junior. They even gave him a scholarship or whatever. He came home just before Christmas and didn't go back."

"You mean he couldn't go back," says Shitty.

"Why not?" I ask.

"Well, word was he got tossed for beating the shit out of some kid. He never said nothing about it. Just came home like it was no big deal."

"You know what he's like," says Paulie.

"I don't think I do," I say.

"Oh, right. Yeah, I don't suppose you do. Trust me—it was totally a Davey thing to do."

"Classic Arsehole," says Shitty.

•

When we were kids, the Royals were everything. We idolized them. I kept whole sets of signatures from Royals players from the mid-eighties into the early nineties. Perspective is weird, though. Back then, as I sat in these same seats near the visiting team's blue line, these players looked like men. Now, sitting here huddled between Paulie and Shitty in a stadium crowded with screaming Pennington locals, they look like the children they are. When did I get so old?

All these kids are between seventeen and twenty and have spent their lives as less than gods, sure, but certainly more than just boys. Or at least more than the boy I got to be. Not that I'm bitter. My high school years were as formative as anyone's, but I look back at that time as a hard-fought victory. I overcame high school. A lot of these kids will grow up and look back at this as the best time of their lives.

Maybe that's how people get stuck in places like Pennington. They peak early and never learn how to try harder or aim higher or do whatever it is that makes the rest of us want to get the fuck out. In small towns, there are two kinds of people: those who can't wait to leave and those who can't imagine being anywhere else. I've never done the math, but I bet a lot of that second group is made up of good hockey players. And then they get older and are forced to take sweaty wads of money from fat guys in fur hats just because it's there for them to take. It's sad and vulgar and makes me wonder if my lack of athletic ability may have been a blessing.

The game is fun. People cheer and boo in response to what's happening on the ice. Shitty passes me a flask and I pour rum into my paper cup, stirring it into the Coke and ice with a straw. The kids play hard. I've watched a lot of hockey across the country, but there's something different about East Coast hockey. It seems more violent. Watching boys slam into each other, swing sticks, and throw punches is barbaric. Everyone here should be ashamed to be spending fifteen dollars for a ticket. I hate that I'm enjoying myself.

When the period ends, the Royals are up 2–1 and I want more of those soggy fries. In the canteen, I bump into Jennifer when I turn from adding ketchup to my gravy-soaked plate.

"Hey you," she says, holding a hot chocolate between dark mittens.

"Oh, hi." Last night I'd been so stunned to see her, I got a bit shy. Between that and Paulie and Shitty refusing to shut up and leave us for a bit, Jennifer and I didn't get much further than basic pleasantries before she had to go.

"Gone for years, then two days in a row. It's really all or nothing with you," she says.

"Yeah. I like to wear out my welcome, then disappear long enough for people to forget why they don't like me." Having seen this woman naked years ago, it's impossible for me not to picture her that way now. I wish I were more mature than that, but I'm also not convinced anyone really is.

"Oh, I'm pretty sure I remember why I don't like you," she says, and I can feel my cheeks flush. "You dumped me. A girl doesn't forget something like that." She's obviously teasing, and I wonder if this is flirting.

"Yeah, well, I was young and stupid. Don't hold it against me." Before she can say anything else, there is a small person—a boy about eight or ten years old—pulling at her sleeve.

"Mom, can I have money for the fifty-fifty?" the boy says.

Mom? Of course, she has a child. It's the direct result of being pregnant. I'd just never thought it through before. Choices, consequences, harsh realities, and all that.

"Yes, sweetie. But if you win, we split the money," she says, handing the kid a five.

"Who are you?" the boy asks with that directness only kids have.

"I'm Adam. I used to know your mother," I say, pausing a little too long after "your" and using a little too much inflection on "mother."

He doesn't say another word, takes his five bucks, and rushes off into the crowd, ducking under elbows and between legs.

"So," I say, "that's him, I guess."

"Yeah, that's him. Elvis."

"You named your kid Elvis?" I laugh, and then try to cover it with a fake cough. Ugh. I'm such an ass. But Elvis? Really?

"Yeah. Phil picked it, and I was burned out from the whole delivering-a-baby thing," she says. "It grows on you."

I forgot Phil was even a thing. "How is Phil?"

"Well," she says, shrugging, "he's good, I think. He's been gone for a while. Out west."

"Not Father of the Year. Got it."

"No, not Father of the Year," she says, and looks down

at the floor. This isn't a subject she wants to pursue in a crowded canteen over hot chocolate and bad french fries. Or, probably, at all.

"Look," I say, "we should catch up. For real. How about, like, a date? Or not a date, just, you know, two old friends, a couple drinks?"

"I don't know. I'd have to find a sitter. How long are you in town for?"

"Not long. A few days. I'm just here doing…a thing."

"Sounds mysterious."

"It's not. It's nothing." I've been trying to impress everyone with my *Sports Illustrated* bit, and now I am downplaying it to an attractive woman—exactly the sort of person I should want to impress—but I don't want to set expectations too high, here. It runs the risk of making me too disappointing later. If there is a later. I realize that means I care about how this date turns out, which is suddenly terrifying. "How about I buy you dinner and tell you all about it? Tonight, tomorrow, whenever. Or I can come to your place, if you can't get a babysitter."

"That's very nice of you to let me cook you dinner."

"Oh. No, I didn't mean that. I'll bring pizza?"

"How about we go out for pizza and I'll figure out the sitter."

"Perfect." And just like that I have a date, but not a date, with Jennifer Clark.

•

My last year with the Marlies wasn't so special. A bunch of the older players moved on, so there were a lot of new faces. Made for a long season of losing. By the time it was over, I was ready to go home and be with Vivian and get on with my life. Like I said, I didn't think there would be any more hockey for me after juniors, and if it weren't for Joe Hayes, that would have been the case. Joe was an assistant coach with the Marlies the whole time I was there and he always liked me. He was one of those coaches who thought hockey needed to be tough and his guys needed to grind and get their hands dirty. So Joe ends up getting a job as an assistant with the Leafs. Day before I hopped the train back home, he comes by and says he wants me in the Leafs camp—a walk-on, no promises, but he'd make sure I got a fair shake. I didn't have a lot of choices. It was either that or go home and maybe play some old-fart hockey. I owe Joe for more than just the chance to try out, because it was him who pulled me aside the first day of camp and told me to put a beating on Duck Wilkins the first chance I got. He looked me straight and said, "You hammer Duck and you might have a shot of hanging around." See, Duck was the tough for the Leafs, had been for years, but Joe thought he was past useful. I could see no reason not to listen to Joe, so first scrimmage I got hold of Duck and said, "Let's go, old man." He laughed, sure, but he obliged, and I made a real mess of him. That was all Joe needed to convince the people who needed convincing, and before the season started, Duck got shipped to St. Louis. Just like that, I was a goddamned Maple Leaf. I called Viv and Mum to tell them. Sure wish I could have seen the look on Dad's face when Mum passed on the news.

...

I dunno. Dad and I never talked about it. I never really went home again, 'cept the odd short visit, and most of those were so I could see Viv. Dad's heart gave out a few years later and Mum sold the farm. You know, it ain't even a farm now, they covered the land with a subdivision in the eighties. They even filled in the pond I learned to skate on. Wouldn't recognize it now if I was standing on top of it.

...

On the Leafs, I was just a pup. I went from being one of the older guys on the Marlies and back to bein' a know-nothin' rookie. I made friends with Pistol Pete Mackie because he was the only other rookie in the room with me. We got a place together near downtown, walking distance from the Gardens. Pistol liked to hit the town and he dragged me out with him most nights. He'd find the dingiest spots, I swear, smoky holes most people didn't bother with where he could drink gin and listen to jazz music. I didn't much like the music and I don't think Pistol did neither, but he was a big fan of the sort of girls you could meet in places like that. They weren't my type, mind you, and I had Viv back at home, anyways, but Pistol liked those city girls—cosmopolitan or whatever—and I had nothing better to do than follow him around most nights. We'd probably not be given the time of day in those places, 'cept Pistol liked to let everyone know we was with the Leafs, and that'd get us some attention.

...

Nah, it was just a small apartment, one room with two beds in it about four feet apart. It's funny, it ain't all that different than my place now, 'cept there was two of us in it. On the nights he'd get a girl to come home with him, I'd go for a walk or sit in the hall and write letters to Viv.

...

It was near the end of that first year with the Leafs— and it was a good year where I got to make myself home on the team and prove I belonged. I also realized I wasn't likely to be going home much anymore. I wanted Vivian with me, but the thought of getting down on one knee and all that, well, it's just not something I could really see myself doing. So I wrote her a letter just like I done a hundred times: "I'm good, how're you, this is what I ate when we went to play in Detroit" sort of stuff, and I tucked it in at the end: "P.S. Was thinking maybe you'd like to get married to me this summer." I thought I was being cute with her, but she topped me a hundred times over writing back only, "Dear Terry, Yes. Can't wait. Love, Vivian." Wish I'd kept that letter. Damnedest thing anyone ever sent to me. We got married the next summer back here in town. I'd have just as soon gone to the courthouse and do it, but your mother wanted the whole kit and caboodle, and I wasn't about to say no to her. It was worth it. I'm not romantic about much, but it's hard not to be a little sappy about your own wedding day. Have you ever seen the pictures? She was sure beautiful, your mum.

...

So, anyways, we got married and she came to Toronto. We got a small place together and it was a bit of an adjustment for her. By the time she came, I'd been in the city for a few years, but I wasn't much of a tour guide. The other fellas' wives looked out for her, though, and I think that helped. I was busy those early years, we were on the road a lot, and I had a lot of learning to do. Seems silly to have to say out loud, but the guys in the NHL are pretty good at hockey, certainly better than the kids in juniors. I found my place, but I had to work hard to keep it and I had to get better as a player.

...

It's true they weren't really looking at me to be scoring many goals. I'm sure people'd be happy to call me a goon or whatever, but I was never bothered by it. I was a Maple Leaf same as the rest and I helped win games in all the ways I could. I didn't put many in the net, but I did my bit. You know, I've always had a theory about what makes the good players good, you wanna know what it is? Peripheral vision. You know, like seeing out the sides of your eyes?

...

Exactly. I watched the best guys play the game: Johnny Bucyk and Gil Perreault and the Espositos. I played with Sittler and Lanny and later on those kids in New York. I skated with Dionne and against all those Canadiens teams in the seventies—Christ, they were good.

Hell, I was still around when Gretzky first started in the league. I seen 'em all, and you know what they could all do? See out of the backs of their goddamned heads, and that's because they had good peripheral vision. They didn't have to be looking at stuff to see it.

...

No, my eyes don't work for shit. I can see well enough what's right in front of my face, but that's about it. But I had balance, hoo boy, nobody could knock me over. Even now I'd put my balance up against anybody's.

...

Well, I'm telling you again. Balance is what got me to the NHL. That and I could take a punch like no one else. Anyways, I was a Leaf and your mum was there with me and we got comfortable—we made a life and I think it was a pretty good one. The team was shaky, though. Imlach was the coach when I got there, but people were tired of him and he got canned. There was some fighting between some of the owners, though I never paid it any attention. I still wasn't comfortable with my place, you know? Always felt like someone would find me out for a fraud and send me packing, so I just kept my head down and did what I was told. We missed the playoffs a bunch, and the years we got in, we were shellacked and sent home early. You ever notice how a Leafs fan is a bit of a sad sack? Like they're born that way, the feeling of being ready to lose is just a part of them. I think that comes from those years I was playing there. We kept losing and up the road the Habs kept winning. It got inside the fans, I think, and they passed it on to their kids. Made 'em all a bit deranged, if you ask me. They think it's fate or something completely separate from anything we did on the ice. It isn't normal to expect to lose the way people expect the Leafs to lose.

...

Oh, it bugged the hell out of me—all of us—all that losing. But it's not like we weren't trying. All you can do is play your hardest, let the chips fall, or some other horseshit.

...

I'm making it sound bad, but it was really just those first few years. We were losing on the ice and there was the stuff with your mother, but you don't want to hear about none of that.

...

Well, don't forget you asked. Truth is, we had troubles because of you. Well, not you, but that we couldn't have you—we couldn't have a baby. I never really wanted kids. I don't suppose that's the sort of thing a father says to his son, but it's the truth, and probably not something you're too surprised to learn. I just knew I wouldn't be very good at it, and you can keep your opinion to yourself on that. But Viv wanted a gaggle of kids. She was an only child like me, but she'd always dreamed of having brothers and sisters. We tried for a long, long time. She lost a few along the way.

...

Yeah, miscarriages. Always pretty early on, but each one harder on her than the last. Killed me to see her sad like that. We never spoke about giving up on trying, but somewhere along the way I guess we made our peace with it. Eventually things got easier between us. I can't say exactly when, but we figured out how to get on and be happy. We'd take trips to Florida in the summer and found ways to keep busy when I was in town during the season. We had a lot of fun those years in Toronto, and even the team got a bit better. We didn't win no Cups, but we were respectable near the end, I think. It was a good time, so when I was eventually traded, it came as a bit of a shock to us.

CHAPTER FIVE

I can't find my mother's grave. We buried her in the back row, but it looks like the cemetery has added several rows in the years since. Pennington has been burying people here for nearly a hundred years. What happens when they run out of room?

We buried her on an unusually hot day in May—me sweating in my suit, noticeably too small, tight across my shoulders, pant cuffs riding high revealing the white socks covering my ankles. Today, the grass is brown and flat against the cold, hard ground. A thin frost coats everything, making all the gravestones sparkle in the morning light. It would be beautiful if it weren't so depressing.

I finally find her about five rows from the back and farther from the east edge of the cemetery than I remember. Just sort of in the middle, lost in a sea of vaguely familiar names. Maybe she knew some of these people, her eternal neighbours. I prefer to think of her spending forever near people she might have been friendly with. The stones vary in size and shape. My mother's is plain and grey and square and cold. Entirely unremarkable if you didn't know the person beneath it.

VIVIAN ANN MACALLISTER

1950–1996

LOVING WIFE AND MOTHER

Loving wife and mother? Who the hell picked that? I haven't been back here since the interment, and this is the first time I've seen the stone. It's the epitaph you use when you have no idea who the person was. It's stock—a placeholder—and unbefitting a single mother. Etched here for a decade and I had no idea. I don't know what I'd have suggested instead, other than something more.

Planning her funeral happened around me—to me, even. People were too nice and too polite, and took care of all the details. I didn't have to deal with anything. I suppose everyone thought they were helping me by keeping me uninvolved. People—some I knew, some I didn't—came and went from our apartment at all hours of the day. They brought casseroles, meat pies, jars of pickled things, and vegetable plates, but mostly they brought egg salad sandwiches. After a day, the pungent egg smell would waft into the apartment every time someone opened the fridge. I can't imagine why people thought a thousand egg salad sandwiches would be any help to someone grieving. Maybe it's just a stage I'm unfamiliar with: denial, anger, bargaining, egg salad, acceptance. To this day, egg smells turn my stomach.

Dave's mother, Carol, spent whole days directing traffic and keeping an eye on me. Not that I was hard to watch over, stuck on the couch as I was. I know the TV was on, but I don't remember watching anything in particular. Occasionally, someone would sit next to me, ask me how I was doing. How was I supposed to answer? I'm completely and utterly devastated. I want to crawl into a hole and wallow in profound sadness until I rot. If bludgeoning you with this remote control and cramming egg salad down your throat until you suffocated would bring her back to life, I wouldn't hesitate. Thanks for asking. How are you?

I just said "I'm all right" a lot.

One of my mother's cousins came by and sat with me for a long time. Until that moment, couldn't remember having ever met him. I know my mother didn't like him. She rarely mentioned him, but I remembered her once calling him "Roger the Twat." He was a small man with thick black eyebrows that didn't cooperate with the rest of his face. When he was sad, they made him look angry. When he tried to furrow his brow and look pensive, they acted surprised. When he said to me, "You know, everything happens for a reason," they did a little dance, as though he'd just told a dirty joke. Drowning in the kind of depressive nihilist thinking any teenager who just lost his mother rightfully experiences, I told Cousin Roger that I didn't believe everything happened for a reason. Instead, I told him I thought shitty things just happened sometimes, and while that sucks, not everything needs to have a point. Cousin Roger smiled and said, "Well, I guess some people are just more spiritual than others." Mom, you were right—Cousin Roger is a twat.

When people in small towns die, it's an event. Especially when they're relatively young, like my mother. Everyone knew when Vivian Macallister passed away, leaving her poor only child behind. It felt like the whole town came to her wake. Everyone except my father. The stone may read "Loving wife and mother," but I stood alone next to her casket that night, shaking hands with everyone she ever met and then some, as they came to pay their respects. Many told me if there was anything I needed, all I had to do was ask, because that's what they were supposed to do. I nodded solemnly and said thanks because that's what I was supposed to do.

In life, my mother kept things simple. She liked wearing jeans. She kept her long, frizzy hair in a bun with one of those leather things you jam a stick through. I'm sure she owned makeup, but I don't remember ever seeing her use it. After she died, her body was handled (a word I overheard someone at the funeral home use) by J. C. La Marsh & Sons.

I don't know which of the sons "handled" her directly, but he got everything wrong. It was bad enough losing my mother (never mind the vague and unpleasant awareness I was standing only a few short feet from a corpse that seemed to take barely perceptible breaths if I stared long enough), but I also had to deal with the fact that Mom's hair was straight, flattened across her shoulders, her lips and cheeks red with paint, and she was wearing a frilly dress I'd never seen before. She looked ready for a spring wedding, not her own funeral.

Carol spent the entire evening there with me, sitting nearby and offering to get me a glass of water every fifteen minutes. Dave came by the wake with some other guys from school. He stopped at the casket and bowed his head. Then he turned and shook my hand. He'd said nothing the whole time my mother was sick, or at any point after she died. Dave and I hadn't spoken to each other at all from the morning my father peeled him off me.

That my father didn't show up for the wake made people pity me more than they already did. I could see it in their eyes and hear it in their hushed whispers. He didn't show up the next morning for the funeral either. I sat in the front pew at St. Patrick's with Carol, my great-aunt Peggy, and a few random cousins—Roger the Twat among them. Some neighbours who served as pallbearers filled out the row, while the rest of Pennington crowded in behind us. It was a full house for the service. From St. Patrick's, we went to the cemetery to put her in the ground, and that's when I finally cried. I mean, I'd cried before that, but like everything else, I'd cried because of some imprecise feeling that it was what I was supposed to do. But when they lowered the casket into the ground, I shook with panicked sobs.

After some time, the crowd thinned around me, the odd person patting my shoulder before leaving. Eventually, it was just me and Carol. She would have stayed forever, but I told her I wanted to be alone. A few minutes later, I sensed someone coming up behind me. I didn't turn to look, because I knew who it was. Sure enough, my father sidled up into my peripheral vision. I had long stopped spending weekends at his house and, once I'd quit hockey and stopped going to the rink, I hadn't seen him much at all. During my mother's illness, he'd stayed away. When she died, he'd stayed away. He missed the wake, and the funeral service. He wasn't here when they put her into the ground. But during my last private moment with her, of course my father decided to make an appearance.

We were quiet for a long time, staring at the hole. Anyone passing by might have looked at us and thought our pain was equal. But I didn't think that fucker had any right to feel the same as me.

So I hit him.

My father's been punched countless times, and few were as feeble as the one I threw. He was standing to my right, so I wound up my left hand and smashed it into his collarbone. It was an awkward hit; I had no clue how to throw an effective punch—the only fight I'd ever been in was with Dave, and he kicked my ass. My father's eyes went wide with surprise, but he didn't even stumble from the blow. A few seconds hung between us while I waited for him to do anything at all, but he just looked confused, so I came at him screaming, fists swinging wildly. He grabbed my wrists and held them as I struggled to hit him again. Were it not for his gimped hand, he'd have easily kept me at bay, but he couldn't manage a solid grip. I shook my right hand free and swung it with everything I had, this time connecting with his jaw.

"Stop it!" he yelled, letting go of my other arm and taking a few steps back, rubbing his face with his fingers. "What the hell is wrong with you?"

"Where were you?" I asked.

"When?"

But I wasn't being specific. It wasn't about one moment. I was filled with a lifetime of disappointment. "Whenever. Always. Where have you been?"

He just stared, hand pressed against his cheek. I wanted to hit him again, but couldn't work up the strength. I was too tired, too sad, too done with it all. I left him there alone, standing next to my mother's grave wearing a weird mixture of hurt and confusion. It was the last time we laid eyes on each other, until I knocked on the door of his apartment at the rink a couple days ago.

After the funeral, as I was trying to sort out my next move, my bank account unexpectedly filled up with money—just over fifty grand. I was surprised my mother had that much to leave behind, but also relieved. That money meant I was free. My high school decided that in light of my circumstances and good academic standing, I would be excused from my final exams. I already had my St. Mary's acceptance, so there was nothing left binding me to Pennington. I stuffed some clothes into an old hockey bag, made arrangements with good ol' Cousin Roger to store a couple boxes of things in his basement, and left a note for Carol to do whatever she wanted with everything else in the apartment. I probably owed her more courtesy than that, given how kind she'd been to me, but I just wanted to go. I bought a bus ticket to Halifax and, telling no one, left early in the morning just over a week after the funeral.

I thought I'd made my peace with all of this years ago, but now that I'm here, I'm not sure I'm okay with any of it.

I hate that her stone reads, "Loving wife." I hate that she's buried in that dress. I hate that there are no flowers on her grave. I hate that I haven't been here in so long. But mostly what I hate is that I can't remember what her voice sounded like. Not really. I can remember what she looked like, but not how she moved or laughed or sang. The problem with the past is that we're constantly moving away from it. I've been letting her slip away and it took coming back to notice how much.

•

I leave my truck parked on the cemetery road and take a walk. It's Monday morning, a couple hours after most people have gone to work, deep enough into November that the leaves have long fallen from the trees and now linger in clumps like trampled garbage in the empty streets. There aren't many sidewalks along Pennington's residential streets, just road and grass, usually with about a foot of worn dirt separating them. Most front yards dip into shallow ditches that are connected by culverts running under each driveway, warping the pavement after a few years. A good culvert bump guarantees that kids on bikes and skateboards will use your driveway for jumps. A few of the houses here have been painted and others look odd, though I can't place why. They're the same, but different.

The cemetery is only two blocks from the elementary school, so I follow the route Dave and I used to take every day, heading toward our old apartment building. One year for Christmas, our mothers got us each a hockey net, which we set up in a cul-de-sac about half a block away. All the nearby kids would come and we'd lose whole days and weekends and summers playing. Back then, to get from the cul-de-sac to home, I'd cut through a couple yards and go in the back of the building. Today, I stay on the road and stop directly in front of it. Twenty-six Jasper Street is an eight-unit building that's perfectly symmetrical in the front, except for the things people keep on their small balconies—barbecues, chairs, one bike. The balcony on the top right—the one that belongs to the apartment where I lived with my mother—has a small table and chair, and even from street level I can make out an ashtray overflowing with cigarette butts.

After a few minutes, I realize standing in the street staring at a building is a creepy thing to be doing. I start to go and when I look up the street I see Carol walking toward me, a small punter of a dog pulling at the leash in her left hand, a long cigarette in her right.

"I thought that was you," she says, smiling as she approaches, her voice rough from years of smoking. "Even from far I could tell." She tosses her cigarette to the ground, not bothering to stamp it out, and comes in close for a hug. She's shorter than I remember and I need to lean into her tight squeeze. The smell of menthol clings to her hair in the cold and her little dog scratches excitedly at my shin.

"Come in, come in, come in," she says.

•

"You really gave us a bit of a scare, disappearing like that," Carol says.

I'm sitting on the couch in her living room, which has ten more years of crap crammed into it. All the units in this building are identical, but Carol and Dave's place always felt much smaller than ours because it was so full of stuff. There's an unmatched couch and loveseat, a recliner, and more end tables than ends. Knick-knacks cover every surface, loosely grouped by theme: ceramic rabbits, crystal animals, miscellaneous coasters and statuettes and candle holders everywhere. There are busts of funny-looking men lining the wall above me: a policeman, a fisherman, a pirate, a Viking, at least two guys in turbans, and, I think, Friar Tuck, along with a dozen others.

Carol hands me a glass of Pepsi I didn't ask for, so I thank her for it. Her hair is still short, but greyer. Otherwise, she looks mostly the same, including her colourful, flowery blouse. The dog is different. She introduces me to Jerry, who is standing on my lap, trying to lick the condensation from the side of my glass. He looks like an oversized rat, with stringy brown hair, crooked whiskers, and small beady eyes. When I was growing up, the dog that lived here was Brutus, a bloodhound mix with stubby legs and a fat belly bald from dragging along the ground.

"People shouldn't vanish like you did," she says with a scolding tone while settling into the recliner. "We worried about you. You coulda been dead, for all we knew."

"Yeah, I know. I'm sorry I didn't say anything. Really. You did so much when Mom died." Carol nods in agreement, and I understand that all she wanted was an acknowledgement.

"Well, word did get back to us, eventually. You went to Halifax, not Mars. Someone spotted you and let us know." She takes a sip of her own Pepsi, scrunching her nose. "I understand why you left, Adam. It didn't surprise me all that much, I just didn't think you'd stay away quite so long. I was hoping you'd come by when I heard you were in town."

"Dave told you I was back?" Did he tell you he punched me in the face, too?

"David? Ha! That boy doesn't tell me nothing. I just heard it in the wind. There's no secrets here, love."

"I keep getting reminders about that."

"So you've been to see your mother?" This is the sort of thing that's important to Carol. It's not even that she believes my mother's soul or ghost or whatever would know if I was or wasn't there. It's just how people are supposed to behave. Visiting the grave of your dead mother is good manners.

"I just came from there, actually."

"Good, love. That's good." A minute passes with only the sound of ice clinking in our glasses. "So. You don't look married." I get what she means, and she's right—whatever married looks like, it isn't what I've got on. I'm too unkempt and scruffy. I have the distinct look of a guy who doesn't have his shit together. "I assume no kids neither. So what is it you've been doing with yourself?"

I give Carol the same condensed version of my story I've given most everyone else and once I'm done with the highlights, all she says is, "Sounds lonely."

Carol has always been concise and direct. She was that way raising Dave, too. When we'd get into trouble for staying out too late or disobeying teachers or whatever, Carol always gave Dave a very specific punishment: three days without TV, or no bike all weekend, or a straight-up week-long grounding. Crime came with a tangible cost, which made it easy for Dave to choose when he was willing to break the rules. He always knew where he stood. My mother was more free-form when it came to doling out discipline. Guilt was her favourite weapon and she wielded it like a goddamn battle-axe.

"What do you think a fair punishment is?" she would say to me.

Having a good sense of what Carol would inflict on Dave for similar or, most times, exactly the same delinquency, I'd suggest similar punishments to what he had to endure. "No video games for a week?" I'd say, mistakenly inflecting it as a question. Invariably, my mother would narrow her eyes and wait for me to pile on to my own penance. And I would, every single time. "Okay, two weeks?" I'd say, like it was an auction, and she'd nod and that was that. Dave thought I was an idiot for continually falling into that trap.

I don't have a response for Carol calling me lonely. What can I say? She isn't wrong—I am alone, after all. The point-form version of my life doesn't include other people. I stare at the framed photographs sitting on the table next to me. Front and centre is a picture from Dave and Stephanie's wedding. It's cheesy and posed and they both look much closer to the people I remember than the people I've seen over these past few days. They look happy, like a couple of kids in love.

"The wedding was really lovely," Carol says, looking past me and to the photo. "It really was. We had a beautiful day. I'll never understand how those two ended up treating each other the way they do."

"How do they treat each other?"

"It's not my place to say. You can ask David. Much as I'd love to have grandchildren, I thank the Lord those two haven't had any kids. What a mess that would be." Carol's shoulders shrink as her eyes shift from the photo to her drink.

"So how is Terry doing?" she finally says. "I don't see much of him these days. I imagine puttering around his rink keeps him busy." I've never heard anyone refer to the rink as being his before. I suppose, in a way, it is. His name is on the building and his sweat is in the ice.

"He's good," I say. "You know, he's Dad. Same as ever."

"I'm sure he is, but that isn't necessarily good. Your

father's a strange bird. There's a man who you think would be lonely to death, but he seems happy enough with it, I guess. It takes all kinds. Maybe you're like him that way."

I wince at the suggestion, not just that I'm like my dad, but that I'm happy to be alone. I've been conditioned to know that that isn't how people are supposed to be, so it's insulting to be branded that way. It's like being told I'm built wrong.

"Your mother was a bit like that, too, come to think of it. She had you, but I really think she could take or leave the rest of us."

I have never thought of my mother as a lonely person, but I'm also not sure children consider their parents much of anything when they are young. Kids are inherently selfish. My mother died before I was old enough to form a real opinion of her. Looking back, maybe Carol is right. I certainly remember that my mother had time for me—she always had time for me. And I know she went to work and delivered meals to patients' rooms in the hospital each day. But she also spent a lot of time sitting alone, either on our couch or out on the balcony, half reading a Harlequin romance, half staring out at the sky. I don't really know if she ever went out of her way to spend time with other people. Again, I'm discovering that the specifics of my mother—the day-to-day minutiae of her life—are mostly gone from my memory.

"Did she regret coming back here?" I ask. "I mean, did she regret moving back to Pennington after the divorce?" Part of me doesn't really want to know. It's tragic enough that she died so young, but to think that she didn't enjoy her life before that is too sad to think about.

"Of course not, love," Carol reassures me. "This was her home."

•

I was with the Leafs for ten years and the Marlies for three before that. Toronto became my home without me even really noticing it. I suppose I knew there was always a chance I could get shipped out of town, but after a while, you get comfortable. I didn't think about it—none of us players really did—until it happened. Lots of guys had come and gone while I was there, but I didn't think it'd be my turn until the day it was.

...

I wasn't thrilled about it, but Vivian was mad at the team, at me, at the league. Hell, I think she was mad at hockey itself. Which was fair—she didn't ask to be in Toronto, so once she found herself liking it, she was mad that someone else was telling her she had to leave.

...

Well, nobody likes being told what to do, do they? Ended up it didn't matter. Sure, I missed the guys and the city. I even missed the uniform—Leafs always did have sharp sweaters—but we loved it in New York almost right away, both of us. It was a surprise, but there you go.

...

Playing with the Islanders isn't like playing with the Rangers. We weren't in New York proper, but out in Nassau. We got a real house with a yard and some space, but we were still close to the city, too. Best of both worlds, I guess. The team was only there because someone got it in his head to start another hockey league—they called it the World Hockey Association and set it up to compete with the NHL. It seemed like a fool idea to me, but they actually stole a few of the guys I was on the Leafs with—some guys were just unhappy, others got more money. I never had to choose between the NHL and the WHA because truth is, no one ever called and asked me to make the jump. The NHL got a bit nervous about the whole thing, though, which is why the Islanders even existed. The WHA wanted a team in New York, where the NHL already had the Rangers. Long Island was the logical spot, so the NHL put in the Islanders to block anyone else from moving in. But the folks who ran that Isles team were smart sons of bitches and put together a real good team real quick.

...

Well, it was different being an Islander than being a Leaf. I was older, for one. I don't just mean I'd aged, but I was a little bit older than most of the other players. I'd been in the league longer and had experience. And that was one of the reasons they wanted me there—to show the young'uns the ropes. They was just kids, most of them, but we got on well and Viv made friends with some of the wives and neighbours.

...

It was a good little team. More than good, really, but the boys were still coming into their own. They liked the way I came and stuck up for them from day one. Made it easier for them to get around the ice, having me around, because everyone knew that if anyone took a cheap shot, they'd have me to answer to. We won a lot of games and they put together a helluva squad for those Cup runs. It was without question the best team I ever played with—one of the best teams anyone could ever play with. Mike Bossy scored near seventy goals! As a pup! They were all pups, Bobby and Clark and Dennis. But they could fly. I couldn't keep up with any of them, not really, but I kept the other teams honest and that was good enough.

...

I'd say that first year in New York was the best year we had, your mum and I. It was easygoing, the hockey was good, we were as happy as we'd ever been. But then, near the end of it, we found out she was pregnant with you.

...

No, no, I didn't mean it like that. It was just, after all the rigmarole with having babies we'd already been through, it seemed like we were headed to the same result and I didn't want that for her again. It was hard on her and that was hard on me. Because it was such a surprise, it really filled your mother with hope, and I didn't want to see her crushed. But it all went smooth, no problems at all. And she was good at it, good at being pregnant and then good at being a mother. She seemed to understand every goddamned peep you made. I was useless, but that didn't seem to matter because she was such a natural. I'd forgotten how badly she wanted a baby, but once she had you it was clear she'd been ready for it for a long time. She was happier than I'd ever known her.

...

Well, we both were happy. Her with you and me with the team. The early years of the Islanders were a bridge between Lafleur and the Habs and Gretzky's Oilers, but we were as good as both of them. Better even. We cleared a hundred points every year I was there, which was a helluva change after coming over from the Leafs. There isn't much that feels as good as winning.

...

You know what happened. I got fucking traded again, to the Los Angeles Kings, of all the goddamned teams.

...

Definitely was a surprise. Mr. Torrey—he was the manager—had the decency to call me himself and let me know. He was the one who wanted to bring me in and he seemed sad to see me go, but we'd been bumped early in the playoffs twice and, coming down the stretch that third year, he wanted a guy who could move the puck a bit on the second line. He thought it was best for the team, and I suppose history proved him right.

...

I cried after that phone call and then I packed my bags to meet up with the Kings on the road in Montreal. We lost that night and again two days later in Pittsburgh. Eventually, we found our legs and limped into the playoffs. Of course it was the Isles there waiting for us. They had their way and my season was over. I got into a scrap with Bam Bam Langevin in the last game, but he was a friend and it wasn't much of a fight. We were bounced, and the Islanders went on to win the Cup. Then the bastards won three more. By the time they got the last one, my hockey days were done.

•

I meet Jennifer at Louie's Pizzeria, which is a Pennington institution. The pizza is crispy, extra-cheesy, heavy on garlic, and legitimately delicious. It's one of the few things about Pennington I talked up to people after leaving, especially at university, where every discussion about food devolved into some version of "My town's pizza joint is better than your town's pizza joint." Not that I ever brought any friends home from school to prove it.

Jennifer looks fantastic in a tight blue sweater, jeans, and brown leather boots. She seems effortlessly put together. I know enough to know that isn't true, that effortlessness is a trick of confidence and well-fitting clothes, but that doesn't make it any less attractive. I finally dragged my suitcase from the back of the truck, with the help of an unsuspecting guest at the motel who had the misfortune of parking next to me, but even with access to my own clothes, I'm a slob. I've always justified my fashion sense as being above the superficiality of brand-name clothing and expensive haircuts, but now I wish I had at least one decent shirt to throw on. Something that stresses my best aesthetic qualities, whatever those might be. At least something with a collar on it. Instead I'm left with the Nordiques T-shirt I picked up at the mall and a navy cardigan. My hair, not used to performing tricks, refused to do anything even remotely presentable, leaving me no choice but to wear my ball cap.

"So I feel like I should congratulate you on the whole mom thing, but I guess it's old news now." I immediately wish I'd said something about how great she looks instead.

"I'm not sure getting pregnant in high school is something you congratulate someone for, but thanks."

"I just mean, you seem to have done alright." I have no idea if she's done alright. She could be a raging crack addict for all I know. "You've done alright, haven't you?"

"It's been up and down, but we manage."

"So what happened to Phil?" I shouldn't ask, but I want to know. "You don't have to talk about it if it's hard or whatever."

She laughs in a way that would make any sane, heterosexual man fall in love. It's all teeth and neck and shoulders, but, you know, sexy. "It's okay. I've had a long time to come to terms with the kind of guy Phil turned out to be."

Has anyone ever had to come to terms with the kind of guy I am? If so, what kind of guy did they decide I was?

"He wasn't ready," she says. "I wasn't ready either, but I didn't have much of a choice. To his credit, he tried for a while. He's in Vancouver now, I think. He sends some money now and then. It's fine."

"Wow. Sorry. That sucks."

"I'm over it. I've had a lot of help from my parents. And Phil's parents, too. I think it's tougher on Elvis. How do you tell a kid that his dad isn't around just because he's shitty at being a dad?"

"I have some experience with this," I say. "I promise you that us kids with shitty dads grow into amazing, successful, well-adjusted adults."

She laughs again and I fall in love again. "Is that what you are?"

"I definitely might be some of those things," I say.

I catch her up on my life: four years at St. Mary's, another one at journalism school in Toronto, an exceedingly dull year interning in Saskatoon, followed by an even duller year and a half in Medicine Hat. Freelancing while bartending in Calgary before finally landing a full-time reporting job nearly two years ago. Is that really the entire decade? I've lost track of how many times I've delivered these bullet points lately, but every time I do it, it feels less substantial. It's a resumé, not a life.

"It's like you've been running away really slowly," she says, noting that each move took me farther from Pennington. "Actually, I should probably thank you. Your disappearing act distracted people from talking about me for a little while."

"People noticed I was gone?"

"Sure. People notice everything around here. How do you do that, anyway?"

"Do what?"

"Disappear for ten years?"

"I don't know. I suppose if you're properly motivated, you can do anything."

"Motivated to do what, though? Just run?"

"Sort of. When Mom died, there was something in me that wanted to get out of here."

"I get that," she says. "I mean, I don't know what it was like for you, but I can see wanting to get away after something like that. I remember how sad it was—how sad we were for you." It's hard for me to imagine a whole town of people feeling bad for that younger version of me, but hearing her say so, I can't help but feel guilty about the way I bailed.

"That was part of it, but I was also very determined to go do… something. I hadn't worked out what at the time. Actually, I'm still not sure I have."

"You wanted to go be successful so you could come back and rub it in," she says.

"Is there a way to say that that makes me sound like less of a prick?"

"Okay, you wanted to prove something to people."

"No, prove it to myself! That sounds more noble."

"Okay, you wanted to prove something to yourself. Very noble. Did you do it?"

"Not yet, no."

"Well, there's always tomorrow."

The waiter—a ginger kid who looks about twelve—drops our pepperoni and mushroom at the table and we each grab a slice. The pizza is just like I remember, a perfect mix of greasy and cheesy, doughy and crunchy, messy and tasty.

"So are you seeing someone?" Jennifer asks after finishing a slice. Is she asking because she's interested or is this just making conversation?

"I was. Sort of, I guess. What does 'seeing someone' mean, right?"

"Did you spend time with them, possibly be intimate with them and do other things with them that you don't do with the other people in your life?"

"Yes," I respond.

"That's seeing someone."

"I don't like to label things," I say. I don't want to explain my relationship with Jana, deciding it probably won't make me look very good.

"Not putting a label on something doesn't actually change what the thing is or isn't."

"It was casual," I say.

"I only bring it up because you seem kind of lonely."

"You know, you're the second person to say something like that to me today. Am I putting out some kind of vibe?"

"It's just, you don't seem to have settled anywhere. A few years here, a few more there. I can't even imagine a life like that. I've got Elvis and my parents and my brother and his kids. I couldn't get away from people even if I wanted to. Your life sounds, I don't know, solitary?"

"Actually, I was going for a lone-wolf thing," I joke, hoping to avoid any deeper examination.

"Oh, well obviously that's working for you," she says.

"It's sexy, right?"

"It's something," she says, and we both laugh.

"What about you?" I ask.

"Seeing someone? Not very often. It gets tricky with Elvis."

Jennifer talks a lot about Elvis in that loving way good mothers do. She took classes at the community college over in Pictou and is now the office manager at the county medical centre. She's spent the last ten years raising a person and working hard to build a full life for the two of them. In the same period, I've been watching sports, writing paint-by-number articles no one reads, and avoiding anything more adult than paying rent. It's not that I haven't lived. I've been over most of the country, seen the Royal Ontario Museum, toured Parliament, and surfed in

Tofino. I had friends in Calgary and my apartment wasn't terrible. I'm an interesting guy (I hope) who has done interesting things (I think), but next to Jennifer—Jennifer who hasn't really left Pennington—my life feels unambitious and small.

As we get to the end of Jennifer's second slice, my third, Stephanie Smith walks up to our table. She's decked out in a stylish black top, leather jacket, and matching leather pants, and is on the arm of a guy I don't recognize.

"Hi, Jen," Stephanie says, leaning in to deliver a quick kiss on Jennifer's cheek.

"Hi," Jennifer replies, awkwardly accepting the kiss. "You remember Adam."

"Of course." She flashes me the smile I wanted from her four days ago.

"Actually, we bumped into each other the other day," I say.

"We did," Stephanie says in a way that confirms that we did, in fact, bump into each other, while also questioning whether anyone has ever bumped into someone else in the entire history of the world.

"Well, I'll let you two eat. Just wanted to say hi." And just like that, Stephanie goes, her unintroduced companion ignoring us as he lumbers by.

"Was that weird? Is she just nuts?" I ask.

"She's," Jennifer says, pausing, "Stephanie."

"And who's the guy?"

"That's Trevor. He's been around town maybe five years now? He's kind of a slime. Works the boats in the summer, sleeps with anyone who's willing in the winter."

"I know first-hand how Dave responds to people saying mean things about his wife." I lift my hat to reveal the bruise in my hairline, which has settled into a dark shade of blue and spread about a half inch onto my forehead.

"You know, I'll never understand why boys think hitting each other is okay."

"Hey—I'm with you. I absolutely prefer not getting punched."

Jennifer looks skeptical and seems genuinely upset I was fighting, which feels unfair. "It's not just that. It's such a guy thing, grown men fighting, and then I have to try and explain to my son how people are supposed to behave."

I can't defend the indefensible. She's right. I do get excited watching grown men fight. I stand and yell and cheer same as anyone, and I have never once considered this terrible behaviour. I decide it's best to keep the focus on Dave and Stephanie, instead of my own questionable instincts.

"That's all fair. I only brought it up because Dave doesn't seem like the kind of person who's going to be thrilled that guy is taking his wife or ex-wife or whatever she is out for a slice of pizza. He hit me because I called her a bitch, so maybe I had it coming a little, but I imagine he'd murder that guy for taking her out. What is it with them? I was with Dave's mom today and she seemed so bummed out about it all."

Jennifer doesn't know who cheated on who first, but Dave and Stephanie have been in an escalating war of infidelity pretty much since they got married. It's something the whole town is aware of and it's continued even into their separation. Besides the emotional destruction to each other, it's led to more than a few fights for Dave, and the breakup of at least two other marriages, but, according to Jennifer, they seem intent on continuing trying to wreck each other.

"That's probably why she stopped to say hi. She's hoping you'll say something about it to Dave."

"Me? She doesn't even know who I am."

"Don't kid yourself. Stephanie is the most calculating person I've ever met."

"So you're saying she thinks saying hi to you is a way to get me to tell Dave about loverboy over there? That's not calculated, that's sociopathic."

"Maybe. Or maybe Stephanie and Dave were just two beautiful people who fell in love and have never really figured out how to be together, so now they go out of their way to hurt each other. They make me sad."

After dinner, I walk Jennifer to her car, carrying the leftover pizza for her to bring home to Elvis. It's a cold night, but she's wearing a thick coat and I'm prepared to stand and freeze for as long as she's willing to talk to me.

"So how long until you run away again?" she asks.

Part of me decides here and now that I'd be willing to stay in Pennington forever. It's not something I say out loud because it's so clearly crazy and probably not even true. You can convince yourself of anything for a very short amount of time, and imagining spending time with Jennifer is easy.

"I don't know. Still working it out." I'm trying to decide if she likes me. I'm not sure I'm even likeable in my current state, but I figure I've at least got familiarity going for me. Sure, she's lived an entire life since the very brief time we were a couple, but people look back at stuff like that fondly, don't they? It's how I think of her, at least.

"Well, if you're around for a bit, don't be a stranger. This was nice." Then she gets into her car and drives away.

Alone in the parking lot, I am still unsure if this counts as a real date, but all I can think is, "You should have kissed her, chickenshit."

CHAPTER SIX

Through most of high school I worked at Perry's Drugs in the Pennington Mall. The uniform included stiff polyester pants and a white shirt with narrow red stripes that looked pink from farther than a few feet away, made of cotton so thin I needed an undershirt so my nipples and back acne weren't visible. Perry's paid a dollar above minimum wage, and working in the town's only drugstore offered fantastic perks. I knew who was buying condoms and who was buying pregnancy tests and who was buying the special shampoo for crabs. I could sell cigarettes to my friends when no one was watching and got deodorant and shaving cream at cost.

Dave never had a job, but he was more than willing to sponge off my disposable income. I let him get away with it because everyone always let Dave get away with everything. There was a liquor store in the mall and I'd get older co-workers to pick us up pints of vodka. Most Friday nights I'd work until nine and he'd wander into the store about a half-hour before close to shoplift candy bars or harass me. His favourite game was to keep an eye on the feminine hygiene aisle for women buying tampons and maxi-pads. When he spotted one, he'd get to the cash register ahead of them and dare me not to laugh, just to put it in my head. Then, as I was ringing up the packages, he'd stand in the distance making faces. I'd have to say, "Sorry, I just thought of something funny," and insert a manual coupon code into the register to give them the sorry-I'm-an-asshole discount.

Dave would meet me outside after I'd cashed out and changed my clothes, and we'd take our vodka to the Burger King parking lot. Depending on what else was happening that night, we'd head to a house party, a bonfire in the woods, or, if his uncle was out drinking, Mac's garage. On nights I knew I'd be drunk, Dave and I stayed at my father's.

One night we stumbled into his place looking to eat some Doritos and finish our pint of Troika. We found my father asleep in his chair and, not thinking much of it, grabbed spots on the couch and flipped the TV channel from sports to Letterman, waking him up.

"What are you doing?" he said, startled and confused.

"Nothing, Dad," I replied. "Go up to bed."

He'd been out cold for a while and his drink was more melted ice than rum and Coke. Still, he picked it up and drank it all. That's when he saw the bottle of vodka sitting on the floor. My dad wasn't a hands-on father, but sometimes he would try to flex his parental muscle out of some sense of obligation.

"What's that?"

Dave giggled and waited to see what I'd say.

"That," I said, pointing at the bottle deliberately, "is liquor."

"No shit, Sherlock. What's it doing in my house?"

"Waiting for us to drink it. Did you want some?"

"No. And like hell you're going to drink that."

"Why wouldn't I?"

"Because I said so."

"What the fuck difference does it make?"

"I'm your father. This is my house. You'll listen to me or else."

"Or else what?" I said, forcing an exasperated laugh.

Dave gave my father the same expectant look he'd given me a few seconds before. He loved watching other people argue. I stood up and stepped close to my father, inviting him to make clear what "or else" meant. He didn't say anything.

"This isn't your house—you don't own it. And you don't get to play the role of responsible dad just because you feel like it right now. As for us drinking, I mean, come on. How many of those have you had today?" I pointed to the empty glass in his hand. "How many bottles you been through this week? Want me to go count them?"

My father bent over, picked up the vodka bottle, and left the room, muttering, "This is my goddamned house," as he went.

I sat back down on the couch and took the chips from Dave's hands.

"That was rad," he said. "I thought he was gonna smack you."

"Fuck him," I replied.

"We're still going to crash here, right? I'm pretty cut, no way I can sneak in without Mom hearing me." He wasn't wrong. Both of our mothers were always on high alert for signs we were drinking, doing drugs, and causing trouble.

"Yeah, who cares. We'll stay here. He's probably already asleep, anyways."

The next morning Dave and I snuck out early, before my father woke up. On the way out, I saw our vodka bottle lying empty in the sink next to an empty bottle of Captain Morgan.

•

Dinner with Jennifer was my first sober night since arriving in Pennington, which is fortunate because Paulie is banging on the door to my motel room at seven in the morning. We are, to my surprise, going fishing. He'd said something about fishing, but wasn't specific about the day or time, so I didn't think much of it. Who fishes on a Monday morning?

These guys do it at least once a month. Mac takes the day off, Dave and Paulie don't often work, and Shitty supposedly negotiated the time off as mental health days, after one of the kids at the school shit in a urinal seven times in one month (the culprit was never caught).

"Isn't it a bit early?" I plead.

"Early worm gets the fish," Paulie says.

"Isn't it too cold?"

"Nah. That helps. Slows the fuckers down."

"Is that true?"

"How should I know, I look like a marine biologist to you? Put these on." He hands me some long johns, a thick hoodie, and a red flannel jacket that smells like campfire and mildew.

"I don't have a fishing licence," I say in a desperate effort to go back to bed.

"Fuck, man, neither do I." So I get dressed.

Shitty is sitting in the front of Paulie's car; I pour myself into the back. They scrounged up extra fishing gear for me, including a pole that jams me in the thigh as I slide around the seat when Paulie takes a hard right turn out of the Goode Night Inn's parking lot.

Millicent Lake is about ten minutes outside town. There are trees around most of the water, with a small, rocky beach on the far side from the road—another ten minutes of walking through the woods—that serves as a perfect squat. When we get there, Mac and Dave are already set up and worming their hooks. Dave casts first and it carries about thirty metres into the middle of the lake, landing with a satisfying plop. By contrast, it takes me about twenty minutes just to get my rod assembled. I manage to get the worm to stay on my hook, but it feels like I'm trying to make the poor bastard suffer as much as possible in the process. My cast is dreadful, landing close enough to shore that I could wade out to get it without having to roll up my cuffs. But catching fish isn't the point. This isn't an intense outdoor experience and we are not communing with nature. There are lawn chairs—old and rusted and full of holes—and two flats of cheap canned beer. The beer, which tastes like pennies, keeps cold in the water at the edge of the lake.

Eventually we are all settled, lines in the water, butts in chairs, beers in hand, silence in the air. I don't think there's any fear of scaring the fish. It's quiet for an hour—no one talks, no one catches a fish, and the only sound is the top popping on another beer. The experience is peaceful, almost meditative.

When the sun clears the top of the trees, bouncing light off the dark, still water, the air changes from bitterly cold to briskly chilled. It's just after nine when Dave hauls the first trout of the day out of the water. Mac and Shitty each get one shortly after.

"So, your old man playing along?" Shitty asks, while Dave reels in his second fish.

"Playing along?" I respond.

"Yeah, playing along. With the interview stuff."

"Sure. Why wouldn't he?"

"He's a strange cat," Shitty says. "Yells a bunch or doesn't say nothing."

"I guess he does. We had a row the other day, actually."

"He used to scream at us to get off the ice if we played shoot around after practice," says Mac. "Loony fucker chased me with a shovel once." He looks over at me, presumably to see if I care that he just called my father a loony fucker. It doesn't bother me because I know he can be. It's nice to get some validation that any conflict with my father is his fault. Everyone knows he's a crazy old man.

It's hard to pinpoint when people turned on my dad, when he went from being town hero to the guy who chases kids with shovels. Probably around the same time he took the job at the rink. He didn't tell me he was doing it. Dave spotted him first, driving the Zamboni between periods at a Royals game.

"Hey, isn't that your dad?"

"Yeah," I said. "They must be up to something."

It wouldn't have been the first time the town trotted out my father for a Royals promotion. I assumed it had to be part of a bigger gag and waited for a punchline, but it never came. My father drove the Zamboni in circles around the ice, leaving a wet trail in his wake. Then he came back with a shovel to clear the small pile of slush left near the Zamboni doors. When he was done, he closed them up, and the teams came back on the ice to continue the game. It happened again following the second period.

After that, my father was at the rink all the time, cleaning the ice, emptying garbage bins, replacing light bulbs, painting and fixing things. It seemed so beneath him, never mind how it affected me—I was mortified. I wanted to ask him why, but instead, I just avoided him. We never spoke about it.

You never really know what your friends' fathers do for a living; you just assume they have boring dad jobs. My dad, for all his faults, had been the exception, which made him cool, and therefore made me cool. But there he was, driving the Zamboni, and everyone sure as shit knew about it. The entire town effectively gathered to watch him do it. Like most kids, I was sure everything my parents did—good or bad—was entirely about me. It took a few years for Terry Punchout to stop being a hero in the eyes of the town. For me, it happened the instant I saw him behind the wheel of that machine.

At midday, Mac fetches a cooler full of sandwiches from his truck. I'm starving and was wondering if we would turn the trout into lunch. This would have been a problem for a few reasons, not least among them the fact that I hadn't caught one. I had a couple nibbles, but every time I yanked on the rod and reeled the line in, all I found was a wormless hook, plundered by fish who'd figured out I'm no real threat.

"Do you screw like you set a hook?" I'm not sure I even get the joke, but Paulie falls over with laughter after he says it.

The sandwiches—roast beef, ham and cheese, tuna salad—were prepared by Mrs. Coleman and are cut into small triangles. They remind me of the food people brought by after my mother died. We've made a sizeable dent in the beer and I should be half in the bag, but the cold air is sobering.

After lunch I wander into the trees to relieve myself. I've always been weird about pissing in the woods. I don't even like urinating in a public washroom if there's someone else in there with me. I look for the right spot to do it, which should be anywhere, but I want to be deep enough in the trees to be completely out of sight. Just as I'm about to go, I hear someone walking up behind me. It's Dave, and he pulls up two trees away. His presence seizes up my entire urinary tract.

"I saw your mother yesterday," I say to Dave, hoping some conversation might relax me. "She seems good. She hasn't changed much, has she?"

Dave grunts in response.

Even when Dave and I were best friends, he didn't say much. Some might think of him as the strong, silent type, but part of me wonders if maybe he just doesn't have anything interesting to say. I want him to be a vapid dummy, because it would give me something to feel superior about. I've been breaking Dave down like this since the day my dad pulled him off my chest, considering every little flaw as a win for me. And now we're pissing in the woods, his marriage is a mess, his good looks are fading, and all he can manage is a grunt for conversation. I know a moral high road when I see it.

"Look, Dave, about the other night," I say. He looks up at me, which is unsettling when I can hear his piss splashing the ground. "I'm sorry about what I said. About Stephanie. I should've kept my mouth shut." I am an amazing and benevolent man.

Dave finishes pissing, zips up, and turns to leave. "It's cool," he says. "Don't leave your dingus hanging out in this cold too long."

It's cool? Does he think that's an apology for punching me? Is it an apology for punching me?

"Um, yeah," I call behind me. "It's cool." I guess.

•

They shouldn't have any hockey in Los Angeles. I truly believe that. It's too goddamned hot and too goddamned fancy, if you ask me. Not sure how I managed to last there as long as I did. You know, I was there for almost three years and never once met a movie star? Not one. I once saw Burt Reynolds in New York and I met that funny guy from TV in Toronto while eating dinner one night, but not a single goddamned movie star in Hollywood. Some place.

...

*The team wasn't bad. They weren't the Islanders, but
they had the Triple Crown Line and those guys were
really good hockey players. Marcel was great and the
other two could keep up with him fine, but for whatever
reason we were a bit of a mess on the ice. I suppose
they'd call it bad team chemistry or some horseshit. It
don't matter what you call it, we just stunk.*

...

*Yeah, I got my record while I was there. Didn't feel right
doing it in that godawful purple jersey, but we don't get
to choose these things. There was sort of a small thing
made about it, but nothing much. I mean, people talked, but we didn't have a ceremony or anything. Nobody
gave me a gold hockey stick. When guys get a thousand
points or fifty goals or something like that, they always
get to keep the puck. There's nothing to keep for the penalty record. I suppose I should have asked for the referee
to give me his whistle. Jimmy Fox joked I should get to
take the whole penalty box home with me. The boys
took me out for a drink, though, and I'd be lying if I said
I wasn't a little proud of it, even if things were a bit shit
for me around then. I was hardly getting any playing
time that last year, then I got hurt, and that was that.*

...

*It wasn't the same anymore after the trade. I had a home
in Toronto and New York, but it never felt like I fit with
the Kings. I was never much for scoring goals, but I'd*

get a few through the year—pucks bouncing in off my arse usually. But I think I only scored twice in my whole time with the Kings. I lost a step and wasn't much use to the team and I was foul about it. It changed the way I played. I never went looking for a fight before then, it was always fighting with a purpose: keeping guys honest, shifting momentum, protecting guys, intimidating the other team, stuff like that. That was my job. But near the end there, I was just spoiling to go with anyone. I'd chase guys down, throw dirty elbows, and got a little more creative with my stick use, if you catch my meaning. I think, for the first time in my whole life, I was just another goon.

...

I dunno, maybe life outside hockey made it all worse than it was. Vivian never came to Los Angeles. I wrote her letters, told her about the beaches—she always liked the beach—but she just wanted to be rid of me. I did visit you both a few times, and even then she barely said two words to me.

...

Not sure I could ever explain myself properly. Truth is, you weren't wrong when you said I was a cheat. I did it. I did it more than once. I'm not proud of it, but I suppose it is what it is. First time was in Toronto, when we weren't getting on so well. Like I said, it took us a few years to find our legs together after we got married. And one night I was on the road and out with the boys and it happened. I was sick about it, I really was. But it's funny, how once you get away with something, it's just a little easier to do it again. I thought she didn't know about all that stuff. Anyways, she was mad about having to go to California, told me I should just quit and we could stay put. Not sure what she thought we'd do for money, but she was deadly serious about it. We fought a bunch, about moving and everything really. Stupid things. Eventually we were having a row and she called me on my cheating and I was either too mad or too stupid to just apologize. I really thought she'd come west once she calmed down. But she never did come. She was a lot stronger than that. We left damn near everything we owned in New York. I tried to have it packed up and sent to her, but she wanted nothing to do with it or me. She even told me if I wanted out of being a dad, I could have that. She said she was ready to let me go and never ask for nothing. She said you were just a baby and wouldn't remember me. I could've just got on with whatever life I wanted. What the hell kind of thing is that to say to someone? She should have come west. She might have liked it. The beaches were nice.

...

Next? I got hurt and I couldn't play no more. Fucking Lars and his stupid goddamned visor.

...

By that season everyone was supposed to wear helmets, but they grandfathered us through, so most of us never bothered. It was pretty fucking stupid, come to think of it. Ice is hard as concrete, pucks are flying around, we have goddamned knives on our feet—the league is lucky nobody got killed. But visors, Jesus, visors are for pansies, and Lars was the original visor-wearing pansy.

...

When all those Russians and Swedes and whatevers started coming over, they didn't play right, but Lars was something else altogether. We'd had pests in the league, but Lars was a rat like no other. He'd get you mad and you'd start making mistakes or taking penalties. Which was fine, it's part of the game, but he wouldn't stand up and fight for himself. He was a chickenshit. I fought a lot of guys, but none of it was personal. Hell, some of them were my friends. But Lars Nilsen...I hated him. Truly. Might be the only guy I ever really wanted to hurt. So that night he said something that rubbed me wrong and I got my hands on him.

...

It don't matter what he said.

...

If you must know, he called your mother something I won't bother repeating. He didn't know nothing about her. Didn't know if she was fat or thin or tall or short, and he sure as hell didn't know she'd long left me. His English was shit, but the guys on his team had taught him a few things to say. That's what made him so good at riling people, hurling out insults you could only half understand through that goofy fucking grin of his. Trust me, everyone wanted a crack at him, I was just the guy who caught him. Just lucky, I guess.

...

Nah, he messed up. We were in a scrum and he said what he said and did his little smile, but he was blocked in and couldn't twirl and skate away like he normally did. I spun him and twisted up my left hand in the front of his jersey so he couldn't go nowhere.

...

You've seen it? Like on TV or something?

...

Well, I don't know about that stuff. And I've never watched it. I imagine it looked a lot worse than it was. Most of the blood was mine, ferfucksakes. I know I hurt him, but it wasn't as bad as all that. I dunno. Truth is, I couldn't feel my hand at all. That fucking visor of his. There was a clip on the side of his lid to hold the visor in place. Just a small piece of metal. Anyways, I must have caught it on the first couple punches, and it ripped a hole in my hand pretty good. Damn thing was numb, which was how I managed to keep throwing it. I must have hit him fifty times before they pulled me off.

...

They knew it was bad. They wrapped my hand up in towels and ice and took me to the hospital. I was still wearing most of my gear. When the doc took the towels off, I laughed at the look of it. Damn thing looked like a ham hock. I didn't get scared until I heard the word surgery. *And even then, I figured I'd sit out the rest of the year and heal up. Never even crossed my mind that that was it. It just didn't really hurt all that much. Stitch it up, slap a cast on it, you know? I still can't feel these here fingers or anything across the back, except the scar itches sometimes. I told a doc that once and he said it was probably in my head, like I'm some kind of nut job.*

...

No, I never heard about Lars, but I never asked neither. That arsehole Swede took my career from me.

...

I don't think I hurt him so bad. I hit a hundred guys as hard as I hit him. It just looked bad is all, because of the blood.

...

Well, shit. He had it coming.

...

I had three surgeries to try and fix my hand and none of them did a goddamn thing to make it better. My contract ended and no one else was interested in picking me up. Made sense, I couldn't even hold a stick.

...

Honestly, I never made plans for after hockey. I guess it's like what I said to Dad way back when he asked me what I'd do with myself: "I'll sort it out when I have to sort it out." Well, I found out pretty quick I wasn't so good at sorting it out. I went back to Toronto because it seemed like the thing to do. I talked to the Leafs and the Marlies about maybe coming in to help out, coach or something, but no one seemed all that interested and nothing came of it.

...

I had a long career and made enough money that if I'd been smart with it, I'd have been fine. I met a guy—it was actually a friend of Pistol Mackie's, who I'd been in touch with when I got back to Toronto. He washed out of the league after only a few years, but did alright for himself with his money. Anyways, he put me in touch with this buddy who presented me with an investment opportunity or some such horseshit. We were gonna sell cars. I didn't know anything about cars or selling them, but he said I didn't need to. They could use my name as a draw. Truth is, I still don't even know what really happened. Something about the land deal for the lot falling through. What I do know is most of my money disappeared. I suppose I could have got a lawyer or something, but I was embarrassed and I was tired. I was near forty years old and for the first time in twenty years, I was ready to go home.

...

I was mostly welcomed back. We had a little shindig down at the curling club, and I was looking forward to doing... something. Never worked out what, I guess.

...

Heh, no, your mum wasn't happy to see me at all. She was never one for hiding her feelings about something. Anyways, you know the rest.

...

I don't know what I expected. I don't think I expected anything. Maybe that was my problem, I was just waiting around for something to happen and not making anything happen. Well, something happened alright— Vivian died. We weren't together, but it still broke my heart. It was like losing her twice. She died and then you left, seemed easier just to keep my head down after that.

...

I didn't give up on nothing, I just wanted to be in the background for a while, or maybe forever. You may not approve of how I live my life, but it's mine to do with as I please.

•

My father and I are starting to find our rhythm, but our pace is slower than I'd like.

"You sure you don't want to keep going?" I ask.

"No, no. I've got things to do."

We're in the Zamboni room, sitting on milk crates. His joints creak as he gets to his feet. When we start these interviews, he seems enthusiastic to talk, but it takes a toll on him. By the end of each session, his pauses get longer and he goes missing inside his own thoughts. Digging through his past leaves him spent, and this session seemed particularly exhausting. I'd let him rest, but there's something that's been on my mind.

"Can I ask you something?"

"Jesus, isn't that all you've been doing?"

"Separate from that. Tape's off. It's just...when was the last time you set foot outside this building?"

My father stands unnaturally still, his eyes fixed on mine.

"It was just a hunch," I say. "I've been here nearly a week and you haven't even mentioned leaving. It doesn't seem like a great way to live."

"You don't get to decide how I live," he snaps, startling me enough that I take a step back.

"Sorry, I was just worried."

"So now you're concerned about me? It doesn't work that way. You can't vanish and then show up to judge me."

"I can't ignore it, though, can I? Living like this will kill you."

"I've managed just fine, thanks."

"What, eating French fries and popcorn from the canteen? Jesus Christ, Dad, you haven't managed at all. Your life is a wreck."

My father picks up a bucket with some tools in it, tucking the handle into the crook of the elbow above his bad hand. He heads to the door, then suddenly turns and sticks his finger into my face.

"Fuck you, you little shit. You blow back into town acting like everyone owes you a favour, but nobody in this world owes anybody else. You judge me and how I live? What about you? Figure your own shit out before telling me how I'm supposed to be."

He turns and storms out, leaving me alone with the Zamboni.

•

Instead of heading back to the motel, I march upstairs to the bar. I'm shaking with anger, not so much because of what Dad said, but because he was right. I'm not in any position to tell him how to live his life. He lives in the rink? Great. I don't live anywhere.

I expect the bar to be quiet. Instead, I find J.J. Johnstone with five of his guys, Paulie's dad among them, laughing it up in the corner. Mr. Coleman spots me and says something to the group I can't make out. A few of them look in my direction, so I nod politely and start toward the bar. I'm halfway there when J.J. lets out a loud whistle and waves me over. I pause, trying to figure a way out of this and, coming up with nothing, walk toward their table.

J.J. reaches his hand up to shake mine as I approach, but doesn't stand.

"A little birdie tells me you're the Macallister boy. Please, grab a seat and join us."

"Thanks, but I really just came in for a quick drink, then

I've got to be somewhere," I say, jerking my thumb toward the door.

"Oh, come on. We've gathered for one of our infamous bullshit sessions, and I hear you're a sports man of some seriousness. Indulge us old fellas for a few minutes." His face is bright red and when he smiles I notice his teeth are oddly small, with narrow gaps between each of them, like a picket fence.

The man sitting to my right stands and offers me his chair. Another fills a plastic glass from one of the pitchers of beer on the table and gives it to me.

I drink my beer quietly as J.J. and his buddies talk shit to each other about hockey and life. It's not all that different from most of the conversations I've had with Dave and Paulie and the guys over the last week, and, frankly, for pretty much my entire life. They're just men hanging out. Or at least that's how it feels for about ten minutes or so, until someone mentions Bobby Monaghan, and then I realize everyone is looking at me.

"So, what do you think of Bobby Monaghan?" J.J. asks, fixing his beady eyes on me.

"He's fine, I guess," I respond.

"I just mean he's on the cusp of breaking your papa's record. My birdie also told me *Sports Illustrated* is having a Terry Punchout issue. It seemed strange to me, but I suppose it has to do with that."

"Yeah," I answer, though he doesn't seem to really be asking.

"Seems odd to give more attention to the fellow losing his place in the history books than the one gaining it, wouldn't you say?"

I don't answer, and instead take a slow sip from my beer. I can see this is all very deliberate. It's not that he thinks I'll change my mind about writing the story. He just wants to get a rise out of me.

"No offence to you or your father, young man, but I think a man like Bobby is probably better suited for holding records. I mean, he's certainly a better player. More well-rounded. He scored two goals just last night."

"And had a fight," one of the others pipes in.

"Yes, and a good tussle to boot," J.J. says. "He's certainly truculent, but also a real talent. A strong career, and he's got a few more good years in him yet, I figure."

"Sure, he's great," I say, then finish the last swallow from my glass. "I should really get going."

"It's a different game today, isn't it?" J.J. says, ignoring my attempt to leave. "Old Punch sure could brawl, but he was never much of a player, you know?"

"He did alright," I say. "Scored more goals than you or me."

"He did. And he spent a lot of years reminding us of that while taking our charity. That must have been hard for him, though, coming home with his hat out. He was never the biggest fan of this place or the people here."

"Can't imagine why," I say, standing up so I'm looking down at J.J.'s bulbous face. "But from what I hear, you don't have a problem giving handouts to hockey players."

"Excuse me?"

"You heard me." I'm feeling tough, like I could take on the lot of them if it comes to that.

"Yes, I did hear you. But I don't think I appreciate the tone or whatever it is you think you're implying."

I shrug. "I'm not implying anything. Just making an observation."

"What you should observe is the kind of man your father really is. I've known him his whole life, and he's never been decent. I'd even say he was a bit of a bully."

"Like that time he stuffed a dog turd in your mouth," Mr. Coleman offers. J.J. blasts him with a ferocious glare and Paulie's dad's cheeks turn red.

"The point is," J.J. says, "Terry is exactly where he belongs, cleaning ice and emptying trash cans. I don't see how bringing up his glory days for a magazine does anyone, especially him, much good."

"I don't really see why it's any of your fucking business," I say. My father has just screamed in my face, basically telling me my life is as useless as his, and still I feel compelled to defend him.

"No need to get upset. I'm just offering you good advice: I think it's best to leave him be."

I'm pissed off, but a picture is starting to become clear in my head. People have let my father be for a long time and it's been an absolute disaster. Why doesn't anybody—including him—realize that leaving him alone might be the problem? Sparring with J.J. might be cathartic, but ideas are forming in my head and I want to get to work.

"Thanks for the drink, guys," I say, and leave before anyone can get another word in.

•

"Well, shit. He had it coming."

Click. Rewind.

"Well, shit. He had it coming."

Click. Rewind.

I've been listening to this bit of tape for over an hour. There's something in my father's voice, a sadness I've never heard before. It's big and tangible. It's also exactly the thing you zero in on when writing a profile about somebody. This is a hook that'll help me humanize my father, giving readers something to connect to. This is first-year journalism stuff, sure, but it's effective. It makes for a very specific kind of story, but it's the kind of story that actually gets published all the time. It's something I can work with.

"Well, shit. He had it coming."

I pull out my laptop and peck at the keys with purpose. Two hours and thirty-five hundred words later, I've created a written sketch of a man beaten and broken by a lifetime of hockey, fighting, and poor choices. He's lonely and vulnerable. He's swimming in regret, and it could be that hockey—our national sport, so entwined with our sense of Canadian identity—is to blame. And it's bullshit. I never lie and I quote my father accurately, but as a profile it still doesn't resemble the man I've spent the last few days talking to. Not really. How could it? I've got maybe ninety minutes' worth of tape from him and a loose idea about solitude triggered by my conversation with J.J. It's hardly enough to understand, much less adequately convey, who Terry Punchout is. Still, it's a good story. Very good, even. It's my father with dramatic flourish, and that's what writers do: we add flourish. With some polish and the help of a decent editor, it can be a great story. I'm sure of it.

I want to email Dan Parker—my contact at the magazine—right away, but the Goode Night Inn doesn't offer internet and it's four in the morning. Also, I know it's a good idea to take time away and reread the piece with some distance. Trying to sleep is useless, though. I'm too amped up and my mind won't stop racing, thinking and rethinking about what Dan's response might be. Then something else nags at me. A loose thread in my otherwise fantastic first draft.

I listen to the tape again.

"Well, shit. He had it coming."

Click. Rewind.

"Well, shit. He had it coming."

Click. Rewind.

I repeat this a dozen more times and then I pick up the phone. He had it coming. He. I know what I want to do, but I'm not entirely sure how go about it, so I call 4-1-1 for help.

"Directory assistance, how can I help you?"

"Hi, I need to track down a phone number in Sweden."

CHAPTER SEVEN

By the time I get off the phone and add three new paragraphs to the article, it's a little after seven. I grab a quick shower, toss my laptop into the truck, and drive over to Jennifer's, hoping to catch her before she leaves for work. She's surprised to see me, because who wouldn't be surprised to have someone show up unannounced at their doorstep first thing on a weekday morning.

"Why are you here?" she asks with more force than I'd hoped for. "Sorry. That was rude. I'm not good at mornings. Hello, Adam," she says with no trace of humour. "Lovely to see you again after, what, like thirty-six hours? Seriously, why are you here?" She's about half-ready for the day: hair is gorgeous as usual, the little makeup she uses is on, but she's still wearing a housecoat, which I find sexier than I ought to. She seems frazzled and me showing up isn't helping with that.

"Sorry, I know it's early and I should have called. I need to use your computer. Well, your internet. I have a laptop," I say, holding my computer up as if she couldn't possibly make the connection between my words and the object in my hands. "The motel doesn't have web access and I need to send an email."

"Email?"

"Yes. And then I was kind of hoping maybe, if it's okay with you, if maybe I could hang around to see if I get a reply." I sound like a lunatic. I barely know this woman and I've just asked if I can sit inside her house while she's off at work. I know Mac doesn't own a computer and the only other place I could think to try is Paulie's parents, which I quickly relegated to Plan B.

"You want to hang out here all day?"

"I do. Well, until I hear back. I promise I won't do anything creepy like put on your underwear." Jesus, shut up, Adam.

"You know what, it's actually perfect," she says. "Elvis claims he's too sick for school, even though he's very obviously not sick at all." She yells that last bit behind her into the house. "Phil's parents are away and my mother is mad at me right now, so I don't want to ask her. I wasn't sure what to do other than force him to go, but then he'll be a little shit all week. But now you can babysit."

"Babysit?"

"Yes, babysit. You're familiar with the concept? There's a child and it's your job to make sure he doesn't die."

It's not that I dislike kids, I just don't have a lot of experience with them. Plus, I'm pretty sure I want to have sex with this kid's mother. It feels inappropriate to spend the day with him first, which is both stupid and presumptuous, but that doesn't stop me from feeling it, anyway.

"He's nine," she says. "It's not like you have to change his diaper. He's completely housebroken. Those are my terms, take it or leave it."

"Of course. Absolutely. It'll be fun. We'll have fun."

"Great," she says with a smile. "He's eating breakfast. Help yourself to the cereal."

I poke my head into the kitchen. Sure enough, the kid from the hockey game is sitting at the table wearing Montreal Canadiens pyjamas and eating Cap'n Crunch. His hair is a disaster, dark and shaggy, flattened against his skull on one side, sticking out every which way on the other.

"Hi," I say.

"Hi. I'm sick." He doesn't seem all the concerned about me being in his house.

"I heard something about that. Looks like I'm the guy looking after you today."

"Cool. Do you wanna play Xbox?"

"Sure. I just need to send a quick email first."

•

Like any self-respecting kid, I loved video games when I was young. Dave and I would play Nintendo for hours until our mothers forced us to go outside. In university, my freshman roommate had a Genesis with *NHL Hockey* and the entire floor of my dorm sacrificed points on their GPA to the game. We'd lose whole days playing, and a guy we called Tool flunked out because of it. While it's been years since I've played, I thought I could probably still hold my own.

It turns out the reason we, as a society, haven't cured cancer or economic disparity or, really, anything, is because our smartest and most talented people have spent the last several years devoted to video game advancement. Suggesting that the game I'm playing with Elvis and the game I devoted so many of my university days to are related is like equating a gas station pastry with Hamlet because they're both Danish.

The controller is enormous and my hands cramp up in the first fifteen minutes. Elvis tries to explain that the joystick on the left is the player's skates and the joystick on the right is the player's stick. Managing both together requires the sort of hand-eye coordination you'd need to dock a space shuttle or cut out a spinal tumour. The graphics are amazing. I remember blocky guys that vaguely resembled hockey players if you squinted hard. These players look like tiny people living inside the television that respond to my every whim. It would feel Godlike, except I make them skate into each other and pass the puck to nobody. Elvis beats me in three straight games by a combined score of 36–1. In between each game, I check for a reply from Dan, but there's nothing.

In the middle of the fourth game, he quickly goes up 3–0 and finally looks at me. "Do you even like hockey?"

I can't tell if he's really asking or just talking shit. When I was his age, it would have been talking shit, but maybe this kid is more sincere than I ever was. "Yes, I like hockey. Do you?"

"Well yeah, look at the score. And I play on the AAA team and I have the third most goals." Elvis is a smug little shit.

"Just third?"

"I'd have more if they let me play centre. But mostly they make me play left wing."

"Left wing is cool. My dad was a left winger and he played in the NHL."

"As if," he says, voice dripping with derision.

"He did."

"What was his name?"

"Terry Macallister."

"Oh, him. People say he played in the NHL, but I've seen him around the rink and he doesn't look like it. He walks all bent over."

"Have you ever asked him if he played in the NHL?"

"No. He doesn't talk to people, except to yell at us to clean up after ourselves in the dressing room. If he played in the NHL he'd have a billion dollars. I saw a picture of Wayne Gretzky's house in a magazine. It probably cost a billion dollars. NHL players are rich. That's why I'm going to play for Montreal someday and make all kinds of money."

"Well, not all NHL players make a lot of money, especially a long time ago when my dad played. Plus, he didn't score as many goals as Wayne Gretzky."

Elvis is distracted by the conversation, and I manage to score two quick goals. "Watch out now, kid. I'm getting the hang of this."

"Oh yeah, watch this," he says, marching his little red-shirted guy through all my little white-shirted guys and scoring. Then he does it twelve more times and I suggest lunch. I check my email one more time and make us some tuna melts.

"Are you dating my mother?" Elvis asks, his mouth full of sandwich.

"Um, well, we went out the other night, but it was just to catch up. We're old friends. I wouldn't call it dating."

"That's what I thought."

"It is, is it? Why's that?"

"Mom doesn't go on dates."

"She doesn't?"

"Nope."

"Maybe she just doesn't tell you about it."

Elvis considers this possibility for a few seconds, that his mother has a secret dating life to which he isn't privy. "No. If she went on dates, I'd know."

He seems convinced and says it with enough conviction that I am, too. We munch our melts silently for a few minutes and then he asks me, "Hey, can you introduce me to your dad sometime so I can get his autograph?"

•

When Jennifer walks in at about five-thirty, Elvis has switched to handing me my ass in a World War II game that's realistic in a way that makes me uncomfortable, though the kid doesn't seem bothered.

"Have you two just been playing games all day?"

"Is that not what I was supposed to do with him?" I ask. "I don't babysit a lot. Actually, the TV did most of the work. I'd have been lost without it."

Elvis laughs. Jennifer shakes her head, but doesn't seem angry that I've let her only child waste a day of his life. She drops her bag at the door, kicks off her boots, and heads straight to the kitchen.

"Are you staying for dinner?" she calls out.

"Sure," I yell, then quieter to Elvis, "Is your mom a good cook?"

"She's okay."

Leaving Elvis to the game, I join Jennifer in the kitchen. She's making fajitas. I would offer to help, but I'd just slow her down.

"I am a good cook, I'll have you know," she says.

"Heard that, did you?" I ask, hoping I can flash a charming smile and power through.

"I hear everything in this house." She's chopping green peppers. "Thanks again for staying with him today."

"No problem. Really, it wasn't hard. If I'd known kids were this easy, I'd have had a couple myself."

She stops chopping and looks over her shoulder at me.

"Sorry." Don't make jokes about kids, dickhead.

"Mm-hm."

Over dinner, Elvis fills his fajitas with sour cream and cheese. I try to cover for him by stuffing extra peppers into mine. When it was just us playing video games, I wasn't trying to impress him. Now that Jennifer is here, I really want this kid to like me. As a consequence, I've gone from actually being a pretty cool guy, one willing to play games for nine hours, to one trying to seem cool, which is inherently uncool.

"So what's your favourite class at school?"

"I dunno."

"I always liked recess," I say, winking at him. He doesn't laugh, and I fear I've already become lame Uncle Adam.

When Jennifer asks the kid to clear the table, I immediately jump in. "He's sick. I can do it. Besides, I owe you guys for feeding me." They both just look at me and shrug.

By eight o'clock, the kitchen is spotless, and while I'm aware I'm wearing out my welcome, there's still no reply from Dan. It's unlikely he'll respond this late, but I'm not sure what I'll do with myself if I can't check every five minutes. Fortunately, Jennifer spares me the trouble of looking for excuses by handing me a bottle of wine and a corkscrew.

"Here, you start on this, I'm going to put little man to bed," she says.

"Aw, Mom. It's not bedtime yet."

"But you're not feeling well. You're sick. You need your rest. Unless, of course, you were lying to me this morning." She's good. And it works. Trapped in his own fiction, Elvis begrudgingly heads for the stairs.

"Say thank you to Adam," Jennifer prompts.

Elvis stops and turns back. "Thanks, Adam. You can practise on my Xbox if you want."

"Thanks, E. I might just do that."

When Jennifer comes back down about twenty minutes later, I'm drinking my second glass of Merlot and checking for email again.

"You might want to talk to someone about that internet addiction. I hear it can really ruin your life," she says, pouring her own glass from the bottle I left sitting on the coffee table and sinking into the couch.

"Yeah. Sorry."

"Don't be." She sniffs the contents of her glass. "How's the wine?"

"Good, I guess. I don't drink a lot of wine." I leave my laptop open on the desk in the corner of the room and make my way over to sit next to her on the couch.

She takes a mouthful of wine and, with her eyes closed, lets it drain down her throat. I can see the stress of the day exit her body as she exhales. Finally she opens her eyes and looks directly at me. "So, when that email comes, what happens?"

"Depends on what it says. If they like my writing, I suppose I finish the article, collect a paycheque, and try and spin it into more work. If they don't, I have no idea. I guess send it to other places—the *Hockey News* maybe—and hope for the best."

"And there's a chance they won't like it?"

"Yep. Very much." Jennifer lets that sit there with no response, so I take a sip of wine and decide to let her in on my little secret. "The truth is, they aren't even really expecting it. I met Dan—he's a senior editor—at a sportswriters' conference in Vancouver about eight months ago. I accosted him, basically, hoping he could give me some good career advice. He was a nice guy and indulged me over a drink. I could tell he wasn't interested in anything I had to say, so I name-dropped Dad and that got his attention. Old hockey players turn up all over the place, old-timer tours and things like that, but not my dad. Anyway, Dan said it sounded like there might be a good pitch in there somewhere and I should call him about it sometime. I didn't really think he was serious. He was probably just being nice. But then I got laid off and a little desperate. So I came up with an angle for the story and decided to just go for it. I still haven't called him because

I'm too afraid he won't remember me, or that he'd say no on the spot. But I thought maybe if I wrote it first, then he'd see how good it could be, and the rest would just sort of happen."

And there it is. Jennifer says nothing.

"I'm not kidding when I say I don't know what I'll do if they turn the story down, which they absolutely probably will. There's no backup plan. I'll have to go find a real job somewhere."

She smiles at that. "That's funny. My whole life is contingencies and backup plans. Not sure I could handle the stress of no safety net."

"That makes sense. You have Elvis. I must seem reckless to you."

"You seem a bit lost, honestly."

We both take another drink.

"I'm sorry about high school. About us. I know we were seventeen and it was forever ago and it doesn't really matter, but still. I was stupid and embarrassed. Mostly stupid." I'd wanted to say this to her the other night, even though I know it's an unnecessary apology. We were seventeen. But part of me is worried it will haunt me forever if I don't say something.

"It's okay," she says. "I probably owe you. You dumped me, I went out with Phil, and now I have Elvis. Like a butterfly effect or whatever."

"You think it was fate?" I ask.

"I don't know. Maybe it's like that Pearl Jam song from high school. What's the line? 'A small town predicts my fate'?"

"I remember it. I think I still have that CD buried in a box in my truck."

"Fate or not, things happen and you make the best of it. I'm grateful for what I have."

A discussion on the nature of fate is a good segue to kissing, in my opinion. And while it's hardly been a deep discussion, I don't want to be alone at the end of the night again regretting that I didn't give it a shot. So I do.

I'm good at kissing. Girls have told me this. It really is all in the lips, which seems obvious, but a lot of people screw it up with too much tongue. Kissing Jennifer is fantastic. We have both improved at this since high school. I want to involve my hands—caress her cheek, brush her neck, and so on—but facing her, my left arm is pinned against the back of the couch, and I still have a glass of wine in my right hand. The kissing continues for seconds or minutes or hours, I can't really tell, but I finally break off so I can get rid of my glass. As I lean back in, she puts her hand on my chest to hold me back, and I hate myself for stopping in the first place.

"We shouldn't," she says.

"Yeah. No. It's fine." Except. "Um, why shouldn't we? Because that was kind of great."

"It was—don't get me wrong. It's not unappealing or anything." Hey, there's something every guy longs to hear: You are not unappealing. "It's just it doesn't really work. For me."

"I'm not sure I'm following."

"Any second you could get an email and be gone. Or you could not get an email and still be gone. And that's okay. Really. But it doesn't work with my life. You said it yourself—you don't have a backup plan. Things in my life need to be more concrete than that for Elvis. And for me."

"Right. That makes sense," I say. "It's very practical and I should probably learn from your example." I think about the other night and how I was so sure I'd stay here forever if she asked me to. But it's not fair of me to say that because she's absolutely right about me, and that sucks. "Still, you'll let me be disappointed about it, right?"

"I would never stand between a man and his disappointment."

•

Dan still hasn't replied to my email, but hanging around after being deemed an unfit sexual partner isn't something I'm prepared to do. I make a quick exit, leaving my laptop behind and asking only that she check it in the morning and call me at the motel if something shows up.

Back in my room, I'm dreaming of the myriad ways the night could have gone better, or at least, better in that one very specific way. But I also go through all the reasons she should or shouldn't be with me.

Pros: Not unattractive. Reasonably clean.

Cons: Unemployed. Technically homeless. Limited ambition and dubious prospects for future success. Documented history of premature ejaculation.

A knock at the door saves me from moving past the superficial into listing my real character flaws—the stuff buried in my DNA. I answer wearing only a T-shirt and boxer shorts and am unsurprised to find Paulie standing outside.

"Jesus, man, I'm tired. I don't want to go drinking tonight."

"Hey, Adam. How are you?" Paulie is pale and shifty-eyed, like he's been caught in a lie and is looking for another lie to get him out of trouble.

"What do you want?"

"Oh, I don't want nothing, it's just my dad told me to come get you. Something happened."

"Am I supposed to guess?"

"No. They were out, Dad and his buddies up at J.J.'s. and Punch—your dad—showed up."

Paulie stops talking as though he's finished explaining something.

"And?"

"Well, J.J. was there."

"Paul, can you get to the part I'm supposed to care about?"

"They got in a fight."

"Who did? Dad?"

"With J.J."

"Really?" The thought of my father throwing his gimped fist at a fat, sweaty man is funny to me. "Wow. That must have been a sight."

Paulie chews his cheek. "No, but you need to come."

"Come where? Shit, did he actually hurt the fat bastard? Did they throw him in jail?"

"No. Your dad, he collapsed. They had to call an ambulance."

"Oh." I'm still not sure what Paulie is trying to tell me. Collapsed can mean a lot of things, but I don't want to ask any more questions. I'm not sure I'm ready for the answers.

"Dad says they wrestled around," Paulie continues, "and Punch just sort of stopped and fell over, like he was drunk."

"Is he okay?"

"I don't know."

"Is he alive?"

Paulie's face calms as though he's only just now ready to have this conversation with me. "I don't know."

•

We drive to the hospital and I ask at the desk about my father.

"He's with the doctor," a grey-haired nurse tells me, not

even asking me who I am. This isn't a busy emergency room—they know why I'm here.

"So he's alive."

"He's with the doctor. I'll go see if someone can come give you some more information."

We sit and wait for about half an hour, until a doctor comes out to tell me that my father is, in fact, still alive, and that's more of a relief than I might have expected it to be a few days ago.

"He's had a myocardial infarction—a heart attack."

"Is it bad? Obviously, it's bad, but I mean, relatively?"

"He's stable right now and resting. We need to run some tests to see what the extent of the damage is, and we'll have to keep a very close eye on him."

"But he'll be okay?"

"For now. We'll know more after the tests."

"Can I see him?"

"Not right now," and then he goes.

Paulie stays with me, sitting in the uncomfortable chairs. The vinyl covering makes fart noises every time one of us shifts our weight. These are the only sounds for about two hours. Eventually, a nurse comes out and tells me I can see my father.

The room is tiny and cold. Machines rhythmically beep, click, and whirr. My father has tubes and wires all over him. His skin is chalky. The deep lines on his face are grey. He looks like a charcoal sketch of himself. Looking at him, I'm not so sure he's really alive. I imagine all the possible scenarios. He recovers, and what? I have to stay and take care of him? He dies and there's nothing left connecting me to Pennington. I'd be an orphan, and even though that wouldn't really be any different from how I've lived the last ten years, it wouldn't be the same, either. Would I speak at his funeral? What would I even say?

"Dad," I say quietly, and his eyes slowly open. I have no follow-up, so I ask him how he feels, which is a stupid question. Clearly, he feels terrible. He looks terrible. His lips move, but I can't hear any sound.

"Sorry, I can't hear you," I say, moving in close and putting my ear up to his face. "What did you say?"

He wheezes into my ear, and then I hear a faint command: "Clean the ice."

•

I'm sitting at Mac's kitchen table. It's somewhere between too late at night and too early in the morning. Mac puts a rum and Coke in front of me, and I'm grateful. Paulie brought me here from the hospital, and, thankfully, Mac and Shitty were up playing cards. Dad's keys are stabbing into my thigh, so I pull the mess of them—about twenty or so keys of varying sizes on a large round ring—from my pocket and set them on the table.

If my father had ended up in the hospital a year ago or a month ago or a week ago, people would have been hard-pressed to track me down. There would have been little expectation I'd show up. I mean, sure, I'd have cared, I guess, but I would have felt more distance. But it's not a year or a month or a week ago. Today my father is in the hospital and it seems he expects I'll take over his job until he gets well.

What has changed in the last week? We've spent time together, but it hasn't exactly been quality time. I'm sad my dad is sick. I'm worried he might die. Is that all it takes? Spend a few hours with someone and suddenly they matter? I feel like I've been tricked into giving a shit about a man I've spent years actively not giving a shit about.

"That old man is crazy," I say to no one in particular. "Like I know how to drive a goddamn Zamboni. Who the fuck do I even call about this?" I whack the giant ring of keys across the table with the back of my hand and it hurts a little.

The keys slide to a stop in front of Shitty, who tilts his head and squints at them. "Wait. Are those seriously the keys to the rink?"

"Yeah," I say. "He told me to take care of the ice. Any ideas about how I'm supposed to do that?"

He smiles. "Well, I do have an idea." He picks up the keys and shakes them. "A little shinny?"

"We can't do that," says Paulie. He looks at me. "Can we?"

"I think we can," says Shitty. "I mean, we have keys. That's not technically breaking into the place, so I think legally and ethically we're in the clear."

While using my sickly father's keys to break into the rink to play hockey is objectively wrong, it actually sounds like something I'd very much like to do. Mac calls Dave, and Shitty takes off to go get his skates and an extra pair for me. We all meet in front of the rec centre about a half-hour later with gear, two bottles of rum, a case of store-brand cola, and a bag of weed. "Anything worth doing is worth doing fucked," was how Shitty put it.

None of the keys are labelled, so it takes some work to get into the lobby and then the rink. A few lights are still on, like someone who didn't know where all the switches were locked up after my father was rushed to the hospital, but mostly it's dark and cavernous. It's quiet and, in some ways, I can see the appeal of living here.

We head to the Royals bench to put on our skates. The pair Shitty brought for me are a little tight but will have to do. Dave is on the ice first and quickly blasts a puck into the boards, the thump echoing throughout the empty arena like a gunshot. He always did have a heavy shot.

I'm the last to get laced up by a wide margin—it's been a long time since I tied skates. Doing it properly requires calluses I haven't had since I was a kid. Standing at the gate, looking down at the one-foot drop to the ice, I'm nervous to step out. Should I have a helmet on? I haven't been on skates since I gave up playing hockey over a decade ago. That feels like another life, a life where I knew how to skate. In this life, there's a better-than-average chance I'm going to bust my head open.

And then I almost bust my head open.

My first step onto the ice is a disaster. I glide about a foot and a half on my left skate, but as soon as my right blade touches the ice, it throws my balance off and I execute a 450-degree spin, arms and stick flailing in a manoeuvre that could best be described as a whirligig. None of the guys seem to notice; they're busy passing a puck around at the far end of the ice and firing shots at the open net. Once I get myself stopped, I stand very, very still, leaning a bit to keep my balance while trying to figure out roughly where my centre of gravity is. Slowly, I straighten up, grasp my stick with both hands, and take a deep breath. I push off and it's perfect.

Okay, not perfect. I have all the grace of a drowning cat, but I'm skating. My strides are short, but consistent. As I close in on the sideboards, I cross over, right leg over left. I can hear the metal cutting into the ice. It's a fantastic sound, completely unlike anything else in the world. There's no way to hear that sound and not feel like a champion skater, even if what you're actually doing is skating only by the loosest definition.

Turning again, I am now headed toward Paulie and Shitty and Mac and Dave. Paulie spots me coming and shouts, "Macallister, heads up," sailing the puck toward me. It comes hard, flat, and smooth across the ice. There's a sharp crack as it hits my stick. You're supposed to cradle the puck when you receive a pass, but instead I just run into it, pushing the puck ahead of me. It's not good technique, but it serves my immediate purpose of scoring a goal on the empty net in front of me, which I do with a lazy wrist shot from the hash marks before falling to the ice and sliding into the net myself. Glory be mine.

.

It doesn't take long for my feet to cramp up and need a break. I take a seat on the bench to flex my toes, uncomfortable but happy. It's not like I've forgotten about my problems, but right now I'm willing to accept there are things beyond my control and it's okay to have some fun.

Dave skates over and jumps into the bench, sitting about five feet to my left. He's here for the rum, which he mixes inside an old water bottle and squirts into his mouth. After a few more squirts, he holds the bottle out and I take it. Dave mixes a stiff drink.

"Why do you take J.J.'s money?" I ask after my second gulp. The question has been gnawing at me.

"The fuck business is it of yours?"

"It's not. I just want to know. Why would you let him have that over you?"

"He doesn't have anything over me."

"Sure, he could ask you to hide a body or something."

Dave gives me an are-you-serious look and fishes his cigarettes out of his pocket while shaking his head.

"I don't really think he's going to get you burying people," I say. "But if he did ask you, you'd have to think about it, wouldn't you?"

"That's a hell of an opinion you have of me."

"I'm just trying to understand it."

"He has the money and I don't. Don't overthink it." He reaches and takes the water bottle back from me, as though he has decided I no longer deserve it. "You're a stick, you know," he says.

"I'm a stick?" I have no idea what that's supposed to mean, but I get the sense I should be indignant.

"Yeah. A stick. You don't know that joke?"

"Refresh me," I say.

"What do you call a boomerang that doesn't come back?"

I do know this joke. Everyone does. So I answer: "You call it a stick." I still don't get his point.

"Exactly," he says. "You're a stick."

"Dave, what the fuck are you on about?"

"You think we're all stuck here. That we don't leave, but we do. Most of us do. Fuck, even Paulie got to Pictou and worked the ferry for a bit. But we come back. We're boomerangs. You didn't. You're a stick. You look down on us, but the thing is, a boomerang is a marvel of engineering or physics or whatever. It does exactly what it's built to do. A stick is just a fucking stick."

"And I'm a stick. This is why you've always been such a dick to me? It's a stupid analogy."

"Was I a dick to you?" Dave asks, and I want to high-stick him in his teeth.

"You know you were."

"I honestly don't think about it. You might lie awake every night remembering high school, but I don't. I moved on."

Wait, what? He's moved on? I've moved on. I got out. He hasn't moved on anywhere. I'm the guy who did something with my life. Aren't I?

I sit and stew while Dave alternates between squirts from the bottle and drags from his smoke.

"You know, I went to university for like two months," he finally says. "I took a philosophy class, which was mostly dumb, but the guy—the prof—told us about this thing called solipsism. You know about that?"

"It's the idea that you can only be certain that you exist."

"Right, something like that. You can only be sure of yourself. I like that."

"Why'd you come back?" I ask, and I genuinely want to know. "You could have done a lot of things."

"What things? Where would I go?" He doesn't mean he had nowhere else to go. He's asking why he would want to go anywhere else.

"I know you got cut from the team in Quebec, but what happened to you in Halifax? You're easily good enough to play university hockey."

"They didn't want me," he says.

"You got kicked out. I heard that. You beat up a guy or something. But why?"

"Why did I beat him up?"

"No," I say, "why did you beat him up badly enough to get thrown out of school?"

Dave looks out at the ice. Shitty and Paulie have dropped their gloves and are wrestling each other around, throwing soft punches. Shitty has Paulie's sweater and T-shirt pulled over his head, revealing Paulie's sizable, hair-covered belly. Paulie, blinded by his own clothing, flails wildly. Mac is sitting on top of the net smoking a joint, jeering at the mock fight.

Dave keeps his eyes on them while he talks. "I don't know. I mean, he was a fuckhead. I don't know how they decide who your roommates are, but that school got it wrong. He was from Calgary. His name was Kenneth and he'd get sour when I called him Kenny. Preppy fucker. Skinny and fucking arrogant. Four of us shared a common room with a kitchen. That kid was always on me about being dirty and having the guys from the team over for beers. I came home drunk, and he tried to give me shit about not doing the dishes or some bullshit. I lost it on him. I don't even remember it, except for him lying there bleeding and crying all over himself. Pissed himself, too." Dave takes another squeeze of rum and tosses the bottle back my way. "I knew they'd throw me out. I sat in my room for two days waiting for the police to show up and arrest me, but they never did. No one showed up at all to talk about it. I left anyway and came home."

Dave came home because that's what boomerangs do.

"I think I'm getting divorced," he says after a few seconds.

"From what I hear, that's probably for the best."

"Maybe. I don't know."

"What do you want me to say here, Dave? Do you love her? Go win her back. Be romantic or beat up that guy I saw her with or whatever. I don't fucking know."

"What guy?"

"Does it matter?" I ask.

"No. I guess it doesn't. But if I find out, I'll kick the shit out of him."

"Well, yeah."

•

We're all drunk and tired, but we've scratched up the ice good and the only thing my dad asked was that we clean it for him. I don't know if he was serious or in a near-death fever dream, but it's hard to ignore what could very well be his last request.

It takes a while to figure out how to turn the Zamboni on and work out what a few of the more prominent gears and buttons are for. I ease it out, jerking forward and stopping and jerking forward again as my foot taps the gas. Once I'm on the ice, I fiddle with switches, waiting for the contraption on the back of the machine to drop down so it can shave and flood the surface.

Shitty, standing behind me, yells, "Okay, it's going, start moving," and I push my foot down on the gas and roll forward down the ice. Behind me Shitty shouts, "It's working. I think. Looks right, anyway."

I keep it pointed straight. When I reach the far blue line, I realize that I will have to circle, but I don't know what the turning radius on this thing is. I wait until I'm almost at the goal line and crank the wheel to the right, but I'm way too deep and have to jam on the brakes, sliding a few inches and bumping the end boards. Plexiglas shakes around the entire visitor end of the ice.

"Ferfucksakes, you can't drive for shit," Paulie says, climbing up onto the machine. "Give it here."

Figuring he can't do any worse than running into a wall like I did, I jump off and step away. Paulie looks over everything for a second before yanking on a handle and slowly backing the machine up. He slams the same gear down and lurches forward, twisting the wheel the whole way. He comes out of the turn about a foot away from the boards, which isn't perfect, but it's a damn sight better than hitting them. By the time he's into the third corner, he's hugging the edge like a pro. The rest of us stand in the middle of the ice and watch, stunned by his proficiency. As he drives back to the middle of the ice, he yells orders to move the nets out of his path, then back once he's passed. After about ten minutes he's done and executes a perfect three-point turn before backing the Zamboni off the ice and into its room.

"How the fuck do you know how to drive that thing?" Mac asks Paulie as we bolt the double doors at the end of the ice.

"I'm not a tit. I work road construction every summer. You think this thing is harder than any of those rigs? Plus we've been watching Zambonis drive around for our whole lives. Or at least I was watching. You dinks must have been looking at something else."

CHAPTER EIGHT

It's almost eight in the morning when we finish. The schedule at the rink says the ice doesn't need to be cleaned again until after the preschool skate in a few hours. Paulie stays behind to cover it, since he's the only one who can drive the Zamboni, anyway. We leave him snoring in the penalty box, a hockey glove tucked under his head for a pillow. My plan is to go grab a shower and head to the hospital, but I can't stop myself from driving by Jennifer's to check my email before she goes to work.

"Back for more? You must love getting destroyed," Elvis says as he answers the door. For a split second I'm rattled by his directness, but then I realize he's talking about video games and not anything related to his mother.

"Not sure you can pull that sick thing off two days in a row," I say with a wink. "Besides, I have a busy day. I appreciate the invite, though."

Jennifer appears behind her son. "Come on, kid, get your shoes on or you're going to miss the bus." She looks at me with an enthusiastic smile. It seems inappropriate, given how thoroughly she rejected me last night. "I thought you might come by this morning," she says, then she frowns. "Are you stoned right now?"

"No. I mean, I was out, but we..." I stop talking as it dawns on me that I've just proved that all her apprehensions about me are completely founded. "It's been a weird night."

"I bet. Well, I tried to call you a little while ago. I think you got your email."

"I did? Is it good news?"

"I didn't read it," she protests, then pauses. "Okay, I did read it. A little bit. And yes, I think it's good news. But I have to get to work. Just lock the door when you leave. You'll probably want to use my phone, too. Don't worry about the long-distance."

The reply from Dan is good news. The best news. He liked the draft—loved it, even—if I'm allowed to read between the lines. They want to run with it and I need to call him right away, which I do from Jennifer's kitchen phone.

"Oh, hey," he says on the phone. "Adam from the bar in Vancouver. I remember that, though I gotta say, I didn't think I'd ever hear from you again. I also gotta say, I'm glad you reached out."

"Thanks. So you're interested?"

"Yeah, for sure. It's a good hook, the father-and-son thing. It's a personal story. It's different. The thing near the end about Lars Nilsen is terrific. But we need you to add some stuff. Is there any chance we can get you on a plane to Toronto today?"

"Today? Why today?"

"I want you to talk to Bobby Monaghan, too. Expand the scope of the piece. We made a call and he can do a face-to-face with you this evening, but then the Leafs go on the road for ten days and he'll be harder to pin down. The thing is, we had something else fall apart for January—another hockey feature—so you came along at exactly the right time, but we need to get this done quickly."

"Today is going to be tough."

"I know, it's fast. Like I said—something else fell apart on us, so we're a bit desperate. We can arrange the flight from here, get you a hotel and all that. I'll get another editor working on this with you immediately—there's some stuff we'll cut to make room. It'll be in the magazine right after Christmas. Adding a Monaghan interview will help bring some contrast. You can really get your hands dirty with hockey-fight culture. I think it'll be great."

Dan is insistent and while he doesn't say it out loud, I get the impression my only shot at getting this thing published is to do what he says. It's a tough call, but I agree. I don't see any other choice, especially when he tells me I'll get $5,000 for the story, plus my expenses in Toronto. Once we've sorted the details, I call the hospital to check on my father. The nurse tells me he's asleep, but is otherwise fine.

I leave a note for Jennifer, something thankful, but I hope also apologetic and sweet and maybe a little flirty. But what the hell do I know.

•

Everything I own is once again stuffed into the back of my truck, and for the second time in a decade, I'm slipping out of town. Except this time there's something I need to do. It's the only thing I can think of to make myself feel slightly less helpless.

The large wooden door to the church opens easily, a testament to well-greased hinges. I was last here for my mother's funeral. It's the same, though empty now, giving it an overwhelming vastness. Stained-glass windows depicting steely and grim-looking Biblical characters I don't recognize line both sides of the hall.

I stop and stare into the marble bird bath full of holy water. My reflection is distorted in small ripples on the surface, but it's still pretty clear I look like shit—like someone who's been drinking too much and sleeping too little. I'm not sure what the etiquette is here. I think I'm supposed to dab some water on my forehead, but I have no idea why. I'm not even sure how I know that. Maybe I saw it in a movie? I lightly touch the pool and rub the wet between my finger and thumb as I walk down the aisle, sliding into a pew on my left about midway down.

At the front of the room, Jesus is strung up on his cross and larger than life. It's a gruesome scene, painted blood pouring from the spikes in his hands and feet, the thorns on his head, and a six-inch gash along his ribs. His expression isn't quite right. Instead of looking pained or anguished or even peaceful and serene, Jesus looks uninterested, like he isn't sure what's going on and can't be bothered one way or the other to give a shit about it. He's bored. That makes sense, I guess. If you're the son of an omnipotent being and death is a fluid condition, being crucified might just be a tedious way to spend the weekend.

There's a slot in the back of the pew in front of me stuffed with books and small packages of courtesy tissues. I take out one of the prayer books and flip through it. Like with the holy water, I don't know how this works.

Glory be to the father and son.

Forgive us our trespasses, as we forgive those who trespass against us.

As it was in the beginning, is now, and ever shall be.

Some lines jump out at me, but I'm not sure I can piece Christian aphorisms into something that suits my immediate needs. I've never believed in prayer. I've never even tried it, at least not beyond wishing for minor miracles during sporting events. It seems silly, asking favours of an invisible being, even if you believe in him. Especially if you believe in him. Wouldn't he have more important things to do? The logistics of praying make no sense. God works on a cosmic scale, and even if he did care about the minutiae of our lives, it seems kind of petty of him to make us ask for help. But people have been praying to all sorts of gods for a long time. There must be something to it.

So here I am and I need a favour. A couple favours, really.

Okay, God. If you're listening, I'd like you to make sure my dad's okay. I know he doesn't do much with himself these days and I'm not even sure how I feel about him, but I know I'm not ready for him to die. I can't promise we'll use any additional time you give us well, but just the same, I'd like him to pull through and stick around. Now, if you think that one is a little selfish, you're really going to hate this next request. I need to catch a break. So give me a sign. Something—anything—that points me in the right direction. I'm not even fussy about which direction it is. I can promise that I'll work harder. I'll be less lazy, or, at least, I'll really try to be. But if you could just help me figure out where it is I'm supposed to be and what I'm supposed to be doing, even just a little, I'd really appreciate it.

And, if I can have one more thing, I'd really like it if you could say hi to my mom for me. And let her know not to worry about me. And tell her I'm sorry if I ever disappointed her. But don't tell her about the lack-of-direction thing. I guess that's it.

Um, amen.

It seems rude to just stand and leave, so I sit and watch the Jesus statue. Staring at it is like staring at my mother during her wake, with my eyes playing tricks so I see slight movements that aren't there: a breath, a finger twitch, a deliberate look in his eyes. I am so completely mesmerized that my heart leaps into my throat when I suddenly hear a voice behind me.

"Would be a helluva lot easier if he spoke back now and then, wouldn't it?" J.J. Johnstone is standing in the aisle to my right. He motions to where I'm sitting. "May I?"

I shimmy down the row a couple feet out of sheer surprise and he rests his girth next to me, his sizable ass hanging over the edge of the narrow bench.

"I hate these seats," he says. "Normally I just stand at the back."

I'm too stunned to say anything. I stare at J.J. while he bows his head, eyes closed and hands folded in front of him. His lips are moving slightly as he faintly mumbles something I can't make out. After a few seconds, he opens his eyes and crosses himself.

Shit, I think I prayed wrong.

"I almost went into the priesthood when I was young. My parents encouraged it, but it never felt comfortable enough. A bit like these damn seats. I thought being in the church would make me a better person. Turned out I'm an asshole and was always gonna be an asshole. I don't think it's the same as being a bad person, but felt hypocritical to stick with it."

I remain silent.

"I called the hospital this morning," he says, still looking forward. "They let me know your dad's doing okay."

"He's alive," I say, my words dripping with hostility.

"I had a heart attack, oh, I guess it was about six years ago now. It's not a pleasant thing."

J.J. turns his head so he's looking at me, and I see his right eye is swollen almost shut.

"He did that?" I ask.

"He did. Always had a heckuva punch. Still does, it seems."

"Why do you hate him so much? This could have killed him. You could have killed him."

"Hey, kid, I'm here same as you, hoping someone's listening and can put this right. And it was him who hit me."

"I'm sure you had it coming."

"Well, maybe I did," he says. "I won't deny I have a habit of poking the bear."

"But why?"

"There was a time I was jealous of your dad's talent and career. But that jealousy dried up a long time ago. The truth is, Terry and I never liked each other. We used to fight on the playground back in grade school, though he always got the better of me. Guess we just never outgrew it."

"You're saying my dad is in the hospital because the two of you couldn't be bothered to grow up."

"No. It's just sometimes it's easier to accept the way things are than to try and change them. For what it's worth, I've said a lot of nasty things to Terry over the years without him raising a fist to me, but last night when I made a crack about you, he didn't hesitate."

Great. My father had a heart attack defending my honour. As if my feelings aren't complicated enough right now.

"Just stay away from him from now on," I say, putting on my best approximation of a tough-guy voice.

"I will. I think all of us could use some peace."

I can't imagine what peace might look like for my father. J.J. stands and shuffles out into the aisle.

"Say, are you sticking around town for a while?" he asks.

"I don't know."

"And you're probably a pretty good reporter, working for *Sports Illustrated* and all?"

"I guess we'll see."

J.J. nods warily. "Well, if you are going to be around, give me a call. I can get you a little work down at the *Record* office."

"And then I'll owe you like Dave and God knows who else owes you?"

"You seem to have some opinions about what I do with my money."

"I think you give guys like Dave money because it makes you feel powerful. It's a scumbag thing to do."

J.J. considers my accusation. "I don't pretend my shit don't stink sometimes, kid. I won't deny I take some pleasure in helping people out, but I do it with the best of intentions. Your friend hasn't done so well getting his life on track, so if I can lend him a bit of a hand, what's the harm? Sometimes people need help, and I've never been one to give a hug when a few shekels will do."

"And then you lord it over them."

"I do no such thing," he says calmly, unfazed by my insinuations.

"I don't believe you. You aren't the altruistic type."

"You don't know me or why I do the things I do. And whether or not you believe something has no bearing on whether or not it's true." He waits for a reply, but I can't think of anything clever enough to say. "All the same, if you change your mind about some work, give me a call."

•

I fall asleep before the plane takes off and dream about my mother. She's younger than I ever knew her and pregnant, sitting at my father's kitchen table on Duke Street. She's laughing and reassuring me he'll be home soon. It's never made clear where he is or why we're in his house, but I accept it in that way you do with nonsense dreams. And it all makes me so happy. We are a family in a way I've never known. It's warm and comforting and I'm excited for my father to come home, but he never does, and I wake up when the drink cart bangs my elbow on its way by. I doze on and off for the rest of the flight, but my mother doesn't come back.

When I land in Toronto, I find a shuttle to the hotel Dan has booked for me and, after checking in and getting to my room, call the number they gave me for Bobby Monaghan. There's no answer. I try again fifteen minutes later, with the same result. On the third try, I leave a message with the hotel's number and start to panic a little.

It's just after nine when the phone in my room rings. I yell "Hello!" into it desperately.

"Whoa. Gear down, turbo," says a deep voice on the other end.

"Sorry. Who is this?"

"This is Bobby Monaghan. Who is this?"

"This is Adam Macallister."

"Jesus, guy, I know. I called you. I'm just screwing with you."

"Sorry. I wasn't sure you were going to call."

"Yeah, I got hung up with something. Anyway, if you want to do this now, just come meet me down at Augie's," he says.

"Yeah, sure. What's his address?"

"It's a bar, champ. Just grab a cab, they'll know where it is."

"Alright, I'll head out right now."

"Watch you don't pull a hammy."

.

Robert Monaghan was born and raised in London, Ontario. He spent high school playing prep-school hockey in Pennsylvania, where he enjoyed a lot of success and was generally regarded as a showboat, though his talent was undeniable. In 1987, Winnipeg drafted him in the fourth round. Bobby might have made it in the league on skill alone, not as a star, but at least as a productive third-line guy. But he was big, scrappy, liked using his stick, and was willing to drop the gloves with anyone who asked. He spent a full season in the AHL before being called up to the Jets for their last two games of the season in 1989. He managed a goal, two fights, and fifty-five penalty minutes in those two games, and broke camp with the team the following season.

He stayed in Winnipeg until 1995, when he signed as a free agent with the Maple Leafs and became the unofficial face of the franchise. His point production was decent, though never amazing, but he was a marquee attraction because of his swagger and propensity for staged fights. When someone wanted to step up and face him, Bobby would toss his gloves over his shoulders, slowly undo his helmet, and spin it upside down on the ice like a top. He and contemporary tough guy Kelly Martin engaged in a half-dozen scraps over four seasons that were more antici-pated and cherished by fans than most playoff games. He even played in one all-star game, though he was a contro-versial addition.

Despite playing hard and fighting often, Bobby was blessed with good health, losing more time to suspension than injury. It was in 2002 that people realized he would probably break the penalty record if he could keep playing into his mid-thirties. At the start of the 2006 season, it seemed inevitable—at his usual pace, he'd pass Terry Punchout's 3,994 minutes by Christmas.

•

The cab driver does know where Augie's is. After showing my ID and paying a fifteen-dollar cover I walk in and scan the tables for Bobby. I am so intently trying to find him, it takes me a few seconds to notice the small stage with the naked woman on it. I've been to strip clubs before, but not many. Seeing a woman on a stage gyrating for the guys sitting in perverts' row, while they toss loonies at her, only embarrasses me. I don't mean I'm embarrassed for her or them, but I'm embarrassed by having to see it. I'm kind of a prude. This is a low-rent strip club. It's a dive, dirty and dark, smelling of flat beer and cheap cleaning products. I am sure the cab driver brought me to the wrong place, but when I turn to leave I see Bobby Monaghan, NHL star, sitting in a corner near the exit.

As I approach the table, he says, "You're the guy?"

"Yeah. Adam," I reply, sticking out my hand. He takes it but is looking past me to the girl onstage.

"I was worried you wanted an autograph for a second. Happens more than I like. Who the fuck thinks I want to sign autographs at the peelers?" he asks, shifting his focus to me, still holding my hand. His palms are clammy and his right eye twitches a little.

"I don't know. Hockey fans, I guess."

"Assholes. I'm happy to sign autographs—nobody signs more fucking autographs than I do—but fuck off sometimes, right?"

"Yeah. That's rough."

Minutes pass. Bobby watches the naked dancers, and I try to figure out why we're here.

"So, did you want to go somewhere else to do this?" I finally ask.

"Here's fine. Though, if you mention this place, I'll fucking kill you. Just ask your questions." I laugh at the casual death threat, but he doesn't. He shifts his eyes from a topless waitress walking by the table to me. "No, really. I don't want to fucking find out you wrote I was here. If I do, I can make sure your job—your life—is a lot harder from here on out." His nostrils flare and his eye twitches again. Whether he means harder because he'll sabotage my ability to speak to pro athletes or harder because writing is tough with two broken arms is left open to interpretation.

"No, that's fine. It's not really relevant to the piece," I say. Then, pulling out my tape recorder. "It's just a bit loud is all."

He grabs the tape recorder from my hand with speed and force. I'm startled, but for the first time he softens and smiles at me. Pushing the record button, he brings the recorder to his mouth.

"So. I'll. Talk. Loud." he says, overenunciating every syllable, then he spins the tape recorder down on the table in the same way he spins his helmet before he fights and waves at the waitress.

"Another Bud and four shots of tequila," he says to her, and then to me, "What's your chaser?"

I look at the waitress's eyes, trying not to stare at her nipples, which are large, round, and at my eye level. She has an eighties-style perm and isn't what I'd describe as conventionally pretty—or even unconventionally pretty, for that matter.

"Rum and Coke." I say. "Please," I add, trying to be polite and respectful, but she doesn't give a shit and wanders off to get our drinks.

"So, you're gonna put me in *Sports Illustrated*. You know I stopped doing this shit a couple years ago, but I figure I've got one more contract in me before I retire. My agent says I need to do things like this to maximize my value."

"No, I get it. It's just...I'm not sure what they told you. This is actually a story about Terry Macallister. My editor just thought I should talk to you and give the story some contrast." I use Dan's word.

"Well, fuck. No one told me that. Fucking agent is a piece of shit."

"Right. So, anyway…" I pause as a new song comes on and a booming voice announces a dancer named Vicki to the stage. "You sure we can't just go somewhere else to do this? I promise we can make it quick."

"Just ask your stupid fucking questions, guy."

"Okay." The thing is, I don't have any specific questions. Dan told me roughly what he was looking for, but I haven't given it any more thought. Maybe I assumed I'd just know what to say, but now that I'm here, adding things about Bobby Monaghan feels like it's just taking away from my father's story. Also, I'm exhausted and not at my sharpest. "So, how do you feel about being on the cusp of setting a new record?" I ask.

It's a bullshit question. He knows it and responds with, "Just fucking ducky, tiger. That all you got?"

"Okay. But I mean, what does it mean to you?"

"What do you mean 'what does it mean?'"

"Well," I say, not even sure what I mean, "I guess records are for people who are the best at something. Like, only one person gets to have the most of something. So what does it mean to you to have the most penalties?"

"Records feel great. I feel great."

"Okay, but it's not like it's the points record or something… glamorous?"

"What fucking difference does it make? It's history, baby!" he shouts, thrusting his beer bottle into the air with one hand and slapping the table with the other. The tape recorder jumps, so I grab it and slide it closer to him, imploring him with my eyes to be more careful.

The waitress arrives and puts our shots and drinks on the table. Bobby picks up a tequila shot and nudges one toward me. "Pound it, homeboy." He fires his shot back and bares his teeth while shaking his head emphatically.

I tip my shot back, and it burns its way to the back of my throat. It's bad tequila and my immediate impulse is to gag, but I manage to get it down. I grip the table tightly, trying to make sure it stays there.

Bobby doesn't notice as he drains his second shot and focuses his attention on Vicki, who is awkwardly draped around the pole in the centre of the stage. When I'm sure I won't throw up, I take a sip from my rum and Coke to wash the tequila flavour out of my mouth. Once I've composed myself, I ask, "Where were we?"

"History, baby!" Bobby says, laughing and repeating the same motions. I adjust the tape recorder again.

"Okay, history. But you don't think it's kind of a shitty history?"

"Who's shitty?" he asks, suddenly serious.

"It's just, history will remember you as a goon."

"So?"

"Well, not even just a goon. I mean this with all due respect, but you'll be the gooniest goon who ever gooned."

"Sure, sounds great."

"The thing is, it didn't work out so well for the last guy."

"Oh, he was probably some kind of pussy. I'm rich, you know. Made millions. Records only make you richer."

He's not wrong about being rich. Yes, my father sunk all his money into a failed business proposition, but he didn't really have that much money to begin with. After he left hockey, salaries exploded. Bobby Monaghan's lifetime earnings are nearly $15 million, and while he's certainly near the end of his career, he was right when he said he has one more contract left. In the free-agent market, there's a few million dollars still out there for him and this record makes him more marketable.

"He's not a pussy. He's just, I don't know. He's just had a rough go of it."

Bobby laughs. "Whatever. I don't give a fuck."

He grabs the tequila shot still on the table—which, while I don't actually want it, I thought was mine—and slowly pours it down his throat.

"Don't you think you owe him a debt of gratitude? Without my dad, you might not be here doing whatever it is you do."

"Your dad?"

"Yes." I didn't realize he didn't already know that. Whoever set this meeting up really didn't do their job very well.

"Terry Punchout is your dad?"

"He is."

"That's funny. Look, I'm sorry I called him a pussy, but I honestly don't really give a shit about the guy. Maybe you think this record is a big deal, but to me it's just a few more bucks in my pocket. My agent says it's a great fucking sales tool."

This isn't so different from my father coming back to Pennington as the conquering hero, assuming his reputation would be enough to carry him through. That record was a sales tool for him, too, but he wasn't a good enough salesman to do much with it. Bobby's made himself a side-show, and whatever his next contract is, it'll likely be for more money than my father ever saw in his career. Bobby is playing a completely different game than my dad, and he's good at it. He's self-aware in a way my father has never been, never could be. I don't say anything. What is there to say? Dan thought Bobby would offer contrast to my father. And he does, only because he's such a transparent asshole, and somehow that makes my dad's story just a little bit sadder. If he'd been a bigger asshole, maybe things would have worked out better for him. And then it all clicks for me and I see where the story I sent to Dan went wrong. Bobby Monaghan is a prizefighter—he does it for ego and money. Terry Punchout fought because someone told him to go fight in the spirit of the game, and it worked out alright, so he kept doing it.

I click off the recorder.

"So we're done?"

"Yeah. I'm not sure I needed you for this. Sorry to waste your time."

"Jesus fuck, did you ever just waste my time. I swear, I'm going to fire my agent. Just say I said something smart in the thing. I don't give a fuck. Whatever you want, as long as I look good."

"Maybe I'll write just that—that you don't give a fuck. Who cares, right?"

"Oh, fuck off. Look, I'm sorry your pops is old or sad or dead or whatever. But it has nothing to do with me. If he's shitty at life, fuck him. My life is awesome."

"Maybe he just knows enough to feel a little bad about punching people for a living," I yell, standing so I'm looking down at him.

"Fuck it, whatever. I'm calling my agent. We can have this shit shut down. Nobody gives a fuck, sally. Congrats, now I'm gonna get you fired. Fuck you and your dad. I hope the old fucker drops dead."

I just swing. With every ounce of my being, I swing. Standing tall over him, I have the advantage. I am the son of Terry Punchout, one of Canada's best-known on-ice pugilists, and for the second time in my life, I throw and land a clean punch. And it is briefly satisfying. I can feel skin and bone and everything in between and see Bobby's face contort in slow motion, and if this is how my father felt with every punch he ever hit a guy with, I get why he kept doing it. It's a hell of a shot. And then all I feel is a sharp pain in the meat of my hand between the thumb and index finger. I look down, opening and closing my fingers quickly a couple times, which hurts even more and has a strange clicking feeling to it.

The thing about pro athletes is that they are pro athletes for a reason. Bobby Monaghan's career is not an accident. He is faster and stronger than I can even comprehend. Nothing makes this more clear than the speed with which he clears the table between us, grabbing my throat and firing his fist at me while I'm still pondering my broken hand. I don't defend myself because I barely see it coming. I feel the sticky carpet pressing against my temple, and then only black.

CHAPTER NINE

Everything I am hurts. My ego, my self-worth, my body. Getting beat up—like, really beat up—doesn't feel like you think it would. For one thing, it hurts a lot more. I ache at the cellular level. For another, it's confusing. The last several hours of my life are like a dream. My memory is a series of disconnected flashes, starting with Bobby flying over the table. I remember him hitting me. I remember wishing he'd stop hitting me in a way that probably qualifies as my second-ever serious conversation with God. Someone had questions. My name? My family? My allergies? I heard voices and screaming. I don't know where I am.

My left eye won't open and the vision in my right is blurry. I'm in a bed. The room around me is bright but quiet. Maybe this is heaven. Who knows. I am definitely high on something. That's nice. I let myself drift away because being awake is giving me a headache.

The next time I come around, the high is gone. If they were giving me something for the pain, they have reduced the dosage, because my right hand and my head are both screaming. My left eye is still dark, but my vision is better in the right and, assessing the room around me, I see Paulie slumped over in the chair next to my bed. He's snoring. I bring my left hand up to my face and feel the spongy, swollen skin above my cheekbone. I push on it lightly and groan as pain skewers my brain, eye, and teeth.

"Hey, man," Paulie says, yawning and stretching his arms above his head.

"Where am I?" Paulie doesn't answer, and I know it's because my voice is inaudible. I don't want to talk. I don't want sound bouncing around the sore spots of my skull. I ask again in a whisper.

"It's okay. You're in the hospital, but you're going to be okay. Probably. You've got a pretty bad concussion and you kind of broke your head a bit. How do you feel?"

"How do I look?"

"You look like warmed-up shit," someone offers from the blind spot on my left. I turn my head as far as I can, searching for the disembodied voice.

"Hi, Dave. Surprised you came."

"My mother made me."

"That makes sense," I say, and then I pass out again.

•

It goes on like this for the next twenty-four hours, partially because of the brain injury, but mostly because of the painkillers. Paulie and Dave stay in Toronto and spend their time sitting in the hospital with me. Paulie's parents are paying for their shared hotel room. The doctors tell me I have a severe concussion but should recover fine. I also have a zygomatic orbital rim fracture, which Paulie keeps calling my rim job.

What happened with Bobby Monaghan in the strip club never fully comes into focus, and I have to rely on Paulie's version of events to fill in the gaps.

"Coked to the fucking gills, he was," says Paulie. "It was on the news. He hit you and then he hit a cop. They got him on assault and resisting arrest. Could get him on intent, too. Guy had enough drugs on him to kill a moose."

"He could have killed you," adds Dave. "He was so high, he'd have put his fist through a cinder block without feeling it."

I remember my dad hitting Lars Nilsen over and over and how he couldn't feel his hand.

"On the plus side, it's looking unlikely he'll be breaking any records anytime soon. I imagine the league might kick him right the fuck out."

On my third day in the hospital, a police officer comes by to get my statement and confirms what Paulie told me. Bobby was charged with assaulting both me and an officer, and with possession for the five vials of cocaine in his jacket. He had picked them up from his dealer and then called me to meet him at the club. Shortly after that, the doctor comes in and tells me I can go, though I'll need someone to keep an eye on me for a few days, just to make sure there are no lingering effects from the concussion.

It turns out who will keep an eye on me has already been decided. While I was unconscious, plans were made and all the people in my life conspired to make sure I'd get by okay— not unlike they did after my mom's death. What they came up with was that I'd stay at Mac's and so would my father, who also needed looking after. The idea was we'd take care of each other, so no one else need be bothered with us.

"Jesus, whose idea was that?" I ask.

"Actually, I thought of it," says Dave, adding, "and you should shut up and be fucking grateful about it," with his eyes, if not his mouth.

"Dave, I am genuinely touched." And I am. I don't know if we're friends anymore, or if we ever really were. But sometimes you're stuck with people in your life and you can love them just for that. Maybe that's how being friends works. Right now, I can't see much difference.

"Eat a dick," he replies with a grin.

I sleep the entire flight back to Halifax, doped up on a double dose of pills to offset the extra pressure flying puts on my fractured face. Jennifer and Stephanie are waiting for us at the Halifax airport. Jennifer comes over and touches my face with her hand, slowly turning my head left, then right, taking in the damage.

"Wow. You're a mess," she says.

Dave and Stephanie don't hug. They say a few words I can't hear, she smiles at him, waves to the rest of us, and they go off together.

"What's that about?" I ask.

"Who knows with those two. Give me your keys, I'll drive home."

I dig the ticket out of my wallet to pay for parking at the machine, which spits my card back and is exceedingly polite when asking for an alternate form of payment. In addition to being broken, I am now also broke. Jennifer is gracious in covering the cost without really mentioning she's covering the cost. This is another embarrassing memory I'll carry with me forever.

The two-hour drive back to Pennington is a quiet one. Paulie is folded into the small bench in the back. Jennifer tries to make small talk, but I'm not in the mood and eventually pretend to fall asleep. When we get to Mac's, she wants to help me into the house, but I insist she leave me at the door, while Paulie carries my suitcase in.

"What should I do with your truck?" she asks.

"Take it for now, I guess." That's obvious, though it's not like I'd make her walk across town or call a cab right now. "Bring it back whenever. I don't have much immediate use for it." Even if I could afford to put gas in the goddamn thing, I've got nowhere to go and a pocket full of pills that explicitly forbid operating heavy machinery. "And I'll pay you back for the parking thing," I say before she turns to go. "I guess I owe a few people right now."

Jennifer pops up on her toes and kisses me on the cheek, which should delight me, but I can tell she means it in a sad, sorry-you're-such-a-complete-and-total-disaster sort of way. Also, the kiss hurts my face.

"I think you're good for it. And it's not like you can skip town again," she says, jingling my keys as she backs away. "I'll come see you tomorrow."

.

Leaving my shoes and bag at the door, I wander into Mac's house. Mac and Paulie are sitting at the kitchen table nursing beers.

"Sweet Jesus, look at you," Mac says.

"I'd rather not," I say. "Thanks for letting me crash."

"No sweat. Your old man's downstairs."

I nod and slowly head down. My father is sitting comfortably in the corner of the sectional, his feet propped up, legs covered with an old wool blanket. He's watching *SportsCentre*. He looks tired, but there's colour in his face and he doesn't seem quite so close to death. I'll need at least one more conversation with God, I guess. To say thanks.

"You look better," I say, startling him.

He looks up at me. "You sure as hell don't. You look as though you was rode hard and put back wet."

"That's about how I feel," I say, easing myself into the cushions.

"I'm watching the highlights," he says.

I can hear the TV, but my vision is still blurry and I'm afraid trying to focus on the screen will only nauseate me.

"So, how hard does the bastard hit?" he asks after a few minutes.

I can't help but laugh a little, which causes the pain to

break through the numbness of the pills. "He hits hard, Dad. He literally broke my head."

My father leans toward me, getting a close look at where my face is bruised and swollen. "You know, there's a trick to it," he says. "To getting punched, I mean. You need to sort of roll your head with the momentum." He pushes his own fist into the side of his face and turns his head to demonstrate. "It's like how boxers do. Hurts less because they don't get you flush. That's where that thing comes from."

"What thing?"

"That thing people say. Roll with the punches."

"Right. You know, this would have been some great advice *before* I had the shit kicked out of me."

"Oh, for sure it would have. Kind of wish you'd asked, now that I'm lookin' at the mess of you."

I close my eyes again, because what the fuck can I even say to that?

•

The next week is mostly just the two of us watching TV. Mac comes and goes and doesn't seem fussed that we've taken over his basement. The guys come by and visit in various combinations, but the bulk of the time is just me, my father, whatever television show happens to be on, and a bunch of short, surreal conversations, initiated by him and seemingly at random.

On Monday, while watching the Canadiens play the Flames: "I like this TV. What do they call it?"

"It's a plasma."

"Plasma," he says, as though making a mental note. "Good for watching the games. You can really follow the puck."

On Tuesday, while watching an old war movie starring John Wayne: "Your mother and I never got divorced."

"What?"

"Divorced. We were never divorced. I had thought you knew that until you said something the other day about it."

"I didn't know. Why not? She hated you—I'm sorry, but she did."

"Nah. She was mad at me, alright. I deserved that. But I always thought with enough time she'd take me back. I think she thought that, too."

"So wait, you were still married when she died?"

"We were."

And just like that, several things make perfect sense.

"You picked the gravestone. That's why it says 'Loving wife' on it."

"Of course. I was her husband and she did love me. Even if she hated me sometimes."

"And you made sure I got her money?"

He screws up his face. "Your mother didn't have any money. She was a lot of things, but good with a buck wasn't one of them."

"Sure she did. I got like fifty grand when she died."

"Aye, that was from me—all I had left over. She made me promise to give it to you for school. Was her dying wish."

"It was your money." I can't quite believe it.

"Of course. Where the hell would Vivian get cash like that?"

"I don't know. Life insurance or something."

"If that was the case, you think you'd have got a wad of cash right after she died, what, with no paperwork or nothing? Nobody gives away money that easy. Well, almost nobody."

"I didn't think about it. Everyone else took care of the funeral, so I just figured lawyers sorted it out, or something,

I guess." The feeling you get when you find out somebody who has always let you down has actually done something really substantial for you is difficult to describe. It's sort of like the debilitating humiliation I'm used to feeling, except instead of wishing to instantly disappear from existence, I'm wishing a terribly painful and drawn-out death for myself. I deserve it and then some.

"Jesus, you must have thought I was so ungrateful," I say.

"Not ungrateful," he says. "Though I suppose I did think we were a bit closer to being even for all the things you blamed me for. When your mother died, people were ready to look after you. Carol Arsenault said she'd take you in. I'd have offered to take you myself if I'd thought you'd come. But you were determined to go, so I convinced everyone to leave you be. I arranged the money and we let you do what you needed to do."

On Wednesday, while watching the Leafs (minus Bobby Monaghan) play the Red Wings: "How did your article thing end? What did it say about me?"

"The end needed work. They probably would have made me change it."

"But what did the thing you wrote say before changing it?"

"I don't know, Dad. What's the end of your story? It said that. It said you got stuck here, driving a Zamboni until you die."

"I suppose that's about what almost happened," he says, as though only now realizing how close he'd come to dying. "I'm not stuck here, though. I can get up and go whenever I want."

"Seriously? You were famous once. You had everything and now you live in the fucking rink and this is the first time you've left it in who knows how long. This town made a joke out of you."

"This town saved me. They gave me a place when I had nowhere else. They did the same for you and for your mother. This town took me in and they left me well enough alone while doing it, which is exactly what I wanted. They did me a kindness."

I remember what J.J.'d said about leaving him be. It's weird that it's the thing they both wanted for him, but for completely different reasons.

"How did you end up in a fight with J.J. that night? Why were you even in the bar?"

"I was looking for you. I didn't like how we left things."

"And the fight?"

"How does anyone end up in a fight? He said a thing, I said a thing. I hit him with my left hand. Never done that before. It wasn't the prettiest punch I've thrown, but it did the trick. If I'd died it might've made a nice ending to that article of yours, ending my playing days with one fight and my life with another. Or something like that. You're the writer."

I have to admit, it's not without a certain poetry.

"But what is it with you two? Why do you hate each other so much?"

"Oh, J.J. has always been a right arsehole. Though I s'pose I wasn't so nice to him when we was kids."

"That's really all it is? You didn't get along when you were young?"

"Sure. Why not? I know what he's been saying about me all these years, but nobody ever listens to that nonsense. Can you imagine such a thing as telling people I was bad for hockey because I got in fights? He never had a problem with anyone else getting in fights, just me. Take fights out of hockey and people'd lose their goddamned minds. J.J. never made any sense. He was just a prick, and I've spent a lot of years paying him no mind, even after he had them put in that stupid bar down the hall from me. I can't imagine spending your life so mad at a person. Letting shit like that rot your insides ain't good for you."

My father is right. For all his poor decisions, he hasn't wasted his time being bitter about the past. Or, at least not that part of it.

"I talked to Lars Nilsen the other day."

"How the hell did you manage that?" he asked, as though Lars were from the moon instead of Sweden.

"Took a few calls, but I found him back in the same town he was born in. It's called Fagersta."

"Is the rat Swede still a shithead prick?"

"Actually, he was pretty funny. He laughed when I told him who I was."

"Son of a bitch was always laughing. So did you ask him why he quit? Did I hurt him so he couldn't play no more, or did I leave him scared shitless?"

"You messed him up good, but no. He actually went back because his father got sick. They had a family business, some sort of restaurant. He took it over, got married, had seven kids. One of them runs the place now."

"Just like that, he quit and went home to have kids?"

"More or less. For what it's worth, he said he always knew someone would beat the hell out of him one day. He doesn't seem to blame you for anything. He's happy."

"Son of a bitch."

On Thursday, while watching a home renovation show: "You know, I was thinking about it, and you might be the only person in the world to ever take a crack at both me and that Monaghan prick. I was trying to come up with someone else who might have been young enough when I was playing, they was still around when he started, but so far no one comes to mind. Just you."

"Not sure I'll stick that one on my resumé."

"No, I'm just saying it's funny, isn't it? Not everyone is the only one to do something, you know."

"Yeah, it's hilarious," I say, popping the last of my pain pills.

On Friday, while watching afternoon game shows: "It wasn't that I couldn't leave."

"What?" I ask, confused.

"The rink. I wasn't stuck in the building, or at least, I didn't mean to be. I just didn't have nowhere else to be. After a while, the outside world sorta faded, you know?"

And I do know. Just like I knew what Dave was talking about with solipsism—not the philosophy of it, but the reality. Other people are exhausting, and making the world smaller—letting it all fade out—makes it easier to ignore them. I get it. Hell, I've done it. I'm just not sure it's a great way to live anymore.

On Saturday, my father announces he'd like to go home.

•

I invite Jennifer to bring Elvis by to meet my dad before he leaves, but first I put in a call to Cousin Roger so she can pick up the boxes I left in his basement ten years ago. While they are still in her trunk, I dig through old photos, some of my mother's belongings, and other things I want to go through later when I'm alone to find what I'm looking for—the small white case that holds my old hockey cards. I open it up and flip until I see it: the 1968 Terry Macallister rookie. The card is well-worn because I could never resist handling it when I was young. On the front stands my father, posed in his uniform with a goofy and youthful smile, his pompadour stiff and jet black. His body is cropped onto a garish pink background. 1968 was an ugly year for hockey cards.

I hand the card to Elvis. "Here, you can have this."

"Oh, wow. Really? The old ones are worth a lot of money."

"I don't think it's worth that much, but I bet we can get it signed."

I take him and Jennifer to the basement where my father is still on the couch watching *America's Funniest Home Videos* reruns on TV.

"Dad, this is Elvis. Elvis, this is Terry Punchout."

"Who's this now? This a grandson I don't know about? You sure picked a hell of a time to tell me. My heart's bad, you know."

"He's not my kid," I say, turning red at the suggestion he just made in front of Jennifer. "He's my friend. And he wanted to meet you." Elvis looks up at me, wide-eyed. "Go ahead and ask him, he's harmless."

He smiles and thrusts the card at my father. "Can I have your autograph?"

My dad takes the card in his fingers. "Well, look at that. Handsome devil, wasn't I?"

Before signing the card, my dad starts telling Elvis about the day of the photo shoot and how they used makeup to cover a black eye. "See, if you look closely, you can see my left eye is a little more shut than my right from the swelling."

I tap Jennifer on the shoulder and we sneak up to the kitchen, where I put on a pot of coffee.

"Thanks for that," she says. "You made his day."

"No problem. I think Dad likes the attention. I should have the money I owe you in a few days. *Sports Illustrated* is sending me a cheque."

"It's okay, it's not that much money. So when will your thing be in the magazine?"

"Oh, it won't. Not ever. They definitely can't run my story after what happened, but they felt bad about me nearly getting killed and were probably afraid I'd sue or something, so they paid me anyway." They also offered me more work if I was planning on going back out west, where they needed someone covering Pacific Division teams. I said I'd get back to them, but see no point in telling Jennifer about it.

"That's good. So what's your plan?"

"Well, I was actually wondering if I could borrow Elvis this afternoon."

"You can, but I meant after that. You know, what's your plan?"

"Dunno. But I'll keep you posted."

After an hour I have to pry Elvis away from my father, who seems perfectly content to keep talking to him. "Sorry, Dad, I have work for this kid."

"Work?" Elvis asks. "Where's my mom?"

"Bad news, she lent you to me for the rest of the afternoon. How much do you weigh?"

•

After the week convalescing in Mac's basement and my father's announcement that it's time for him to go home, the town council got together and found the funds to hire him an assistant. Paulie is the only person who applies for the job and, despite some initial protests, my father realizes it might be good to have someone around to do all the shitty things he doesn't like doing.

On the afternoon I borrow Elvis, we meet Paulie and Shitty at the rink and carry my TV and stereo to my father's small room. We use Elvis to climb into the ceiling and splice the cable from J.J.'s bar to hook up the TV. When my father arrived home and saw his new set-up, all he could say was, "That's just lovely, that is."

A few years ago I was watching Don Cherry doing his *Hockey Night in Canada* shtick when suddenly he said, "Everybody should live their lives the way Terry Punchout played hockey." At the time, I laughed. Cherry was extolling the virtues of being a tough guy, and it seemed like such a ridiculous thing to say. I got his point, inelegant as it was, that my father was fearless and dogged on the ice. He would put everything on the line to win. I suppose it's not terrible life advice, but my father has never lived his life the way he played hockey. When he was playing, he was bold and determined and did what was expected of him. Away from hockey, he never found his place or purpose. He let life happen to him; he rarely jumped in to try and shift the momentum. Terry Punchout has his flaws, to be sure, but it's like what J.J. said: being an asshole isn't the same as being a bad person. And I no longer believe my father is a bad person. He's Terry. Good old Punch. He could go years without talking to anyone and still be part of the fabric of this community. That's something.

Without really realizing it, I started rewriting my father's story in my head. What I sent to *Sports Illustrated* was a simple caricature of a man who isn't so simple. I know a lot of things about Terry Punchout, but I don't know him. Not really.

A few days after he goes home, I stop by for a visit and take out my tape recorder.

"I thought that nonsense was done with," he says as I put it in front of him.

"It is," I say. "This is for something else."

"What else?"

"I don't know. Let's say it's for posterity."

He laughs at that.

The truth is, I think knowing his full story is still worth something, even if it's only for me.

ACKNOWLEDGEMENTS

The Team
My eternal thanks and undying gratitude to everyone who helped me get this thing into the world: Chris Turner, Colin Leach, Jill Thompson, Rachelle Pinnow, Laurie Fisher-Zottman, Laurie McCulloch, Felicia Zuniga, Kimberly Gilbert, Robin Van Eck and the Alexandra Writers' Centre Society, Erica Lenti, Lisa Whittington-Hill, *THIS Magazine*, Swans of Inglewood, Adam Bassett, Dr. Pat Walsh, The Banjo Hitters Social Club, Julie Wilson, Megan Fildes, Will Ferguson, Stacey May Fowles, Gare Joyce, Terry Fallis, Sam, Norrie, Thea, Mom, Dad, Rhonda, Sarah, marilyn, and Gordon.

All Stars
Extra special thanks to those who worked directly on the book: Leigh Nash, you changed my life; Carrie Mumford, I wouldn't have got here without your friendship and support; Theanna Bischoff and Lori Hahnel, I'm so, so thankful for your guidance.

MVP
My wife, my partner, my best friend: Käthe Lemon I'll never be able to thank you enough for this book, for my wonderful life and for all that other stuff.

INVISIBLE PUBLISHING produces fine Canadian literature for those who enjoy such things. As an independent, not-for-profit publisher, our work includes building communities that sustain and encourage engaging, literary, and current writing.

Invisible Publishing has been in operation for over a decade. We released our first fiction titles in the spring of 2007, and our catalogue has come to include works of graphic fiction and nonfiction, pop culture biographies, experimental poetry, and prose.

We are committed to publishing diverse voices and experiences. In acknowledging historical and systemic barriers, and the limits of our existing catalogue, we strongly encourage LGBTQ2SIA+, Indigenous, and writers of colour to submit their work.

Invisible Publishing is also home to the Bibliophonic series of music books and the Throwback series of CanLit reissues.

If you'd like to know more, please get in touch: info@invisiblepublishing.com